THE SMURFS
AND THE EGG

Peyo

THE SMURFS AND THE EGG

TAPP
I'll smurf that egg, or I'm a smurfish sausage!
TAPP
But... but what happened to me?

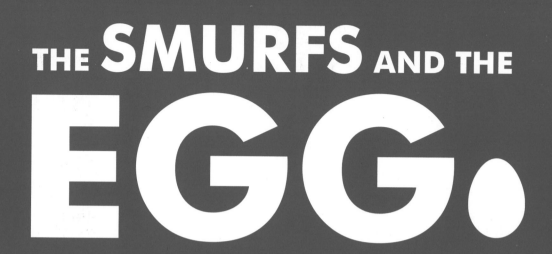

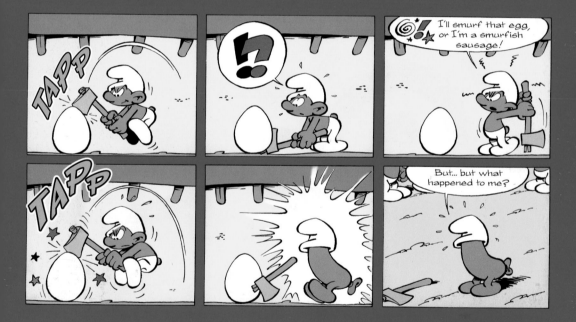

A SMURFS GRAPHIC NOVEL BY Peyo

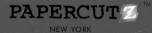

PAPERCUTZ™
NEW YORK

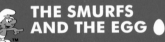

SMURFS GRAPHIC NOVELS AVAILABLE FROM PAPERCUTZ™

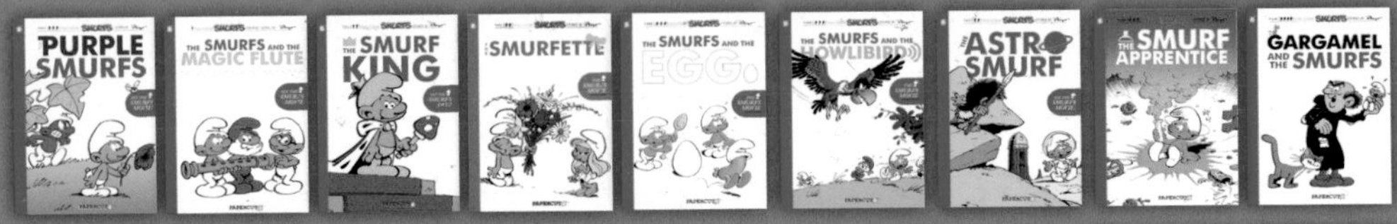
PURPLE SMURFS
THE SMURFS AND THE MAGIC FLUTE
THE SMURF KING
SMURFETTE
THE SMURFS AND THE EGG
THE SMURFS AND THE HOWLIBIRD
ASTRO SMURF
THE SMURF APPRENTICE
GARGAMEL AND THE SMURFS

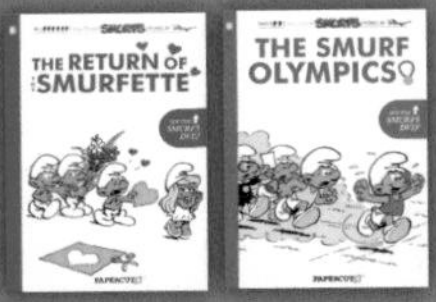
THE RETURN OF THE SMURFETTE
THE SMURF OLYMPICS

1. **THE PURPLE SMURFS**
2. **THE SMURFS AND THE MAGIC FLUTE**
3. **THE SMURF KING**
4. **THE SMURFETTE**
5. **THE SMURFS AND THE EGG**
6. **THE SMURFS AND THE HOWLIBIRD**
7. **THE ASTROSMURF**
8. **THE SMURF APPRENTICE**
9. **GARGAMEL AND THE SMURFS**
10. **THE RETURN OF THE SMURFETTE**
11. **THE SMURF OLYMPICS**

COMING SOON:

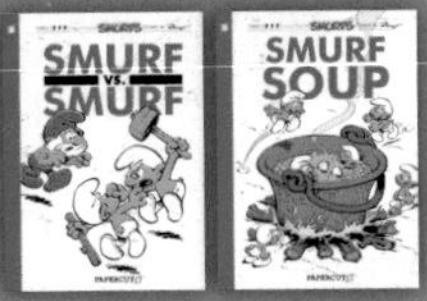
SMURF VS. SMURF
SMURF SOUP

12. **SMURF VS. SMURF**
13. **SMURF SOUP**

THE SMURFS graphic novels are available in paperback for $5.99 each and in hardcover for $10.99 each at booksellers everywhere.

Or order from us. Please add $4.00 for postage and handling for the first book, add $1.00 for each additional book. Please make check payable to NBM Publishing. Send to: PAPERCUTZ, 160 Broadway, Suite 700, East Wing, New York, NY 10038 (1-800-886-1223).

THE SMURFS graphic novels are also available digitally from **COMIXOLOGY**.com.

WWW.PAPERCUTZ.COM

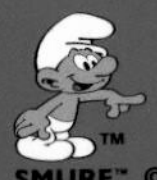

THE SMURFS AND THE EGG

"The Smurfs and the Egg"
BY YVAN DELPORTE AND PEYO

"The Fake Smurf"
BY YVAN DELPORTE AND PEYO

"The Hundredth Smurf"
BY YVAN DELPORTE AND PEYO

Joe Johnson, *SMURFLATIONS*
Adam Grano, *SMURFIC DESIGN*
Janice Chiang, *LETTERING SMURFETTE*
Matt. Murray, *SMURF CONSULTANT*
Michael Petranek, *ASSOCIATE SMURF*
Jim Salicrup, *SMURF-IN-CHIEF*

PAPERBACK EDITION ISBN: 978-1-59707-246-5
HARDCOVER EDITION ISBN: 978-1-59707-247-2

PRINTED IN CHINA APRIL 2012 BY WKT CO. LTD.
3/F PHASE I LEADER INDUSTRIAL CENTRE
188 TEXACO ROAD, TSEUN WAN, N.T., HONG KONG

DISTRIBUTED BY MACMILLAN
FOURTH PAPERCUTZ PRINTING

THE SMURFS AND THE EGG

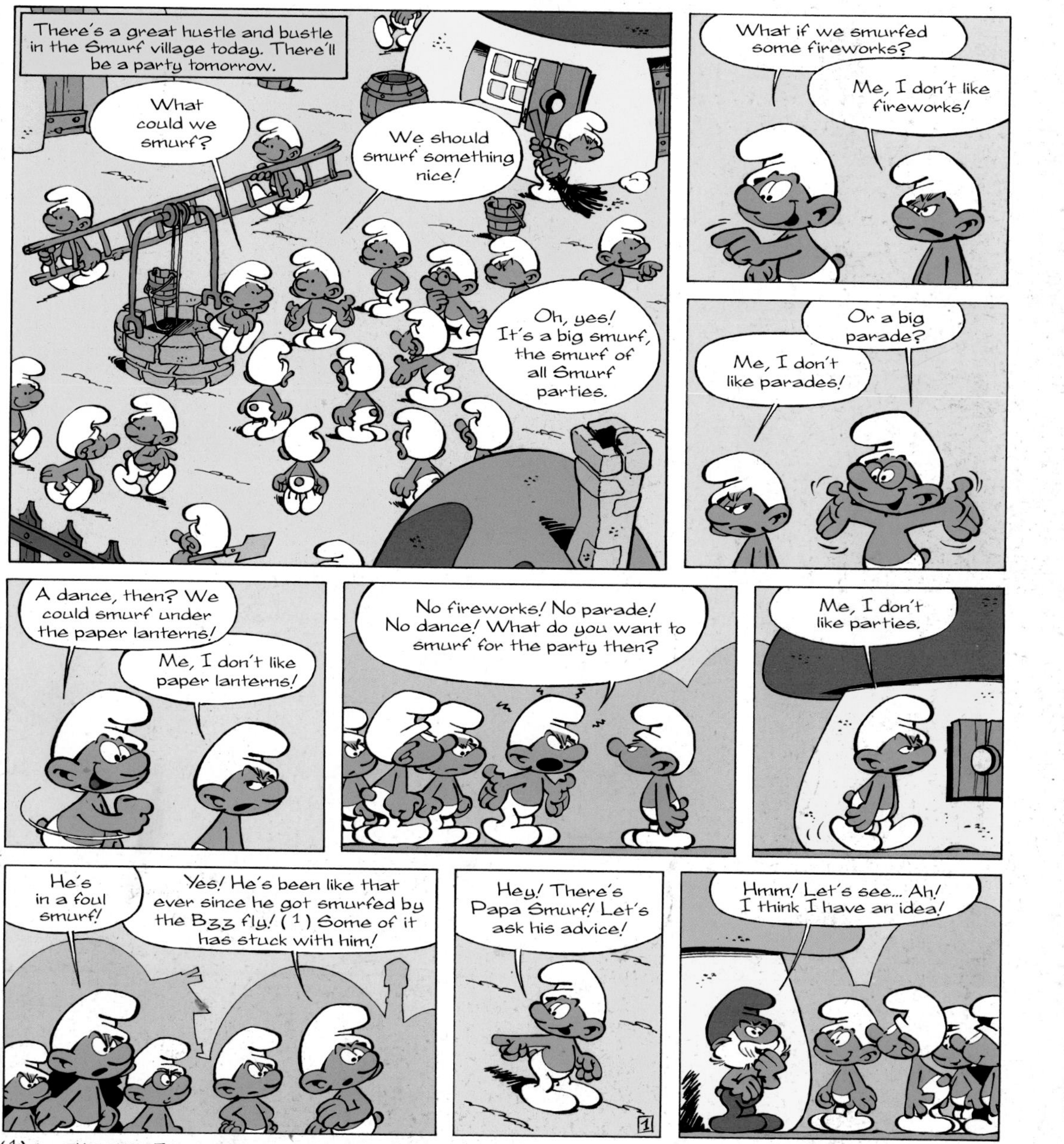

There's a great hustle and bustle in the Smurf village today. There'll be a party tomorrow.
What could we smurf?
We should smurf something nice!
Oh, yes! It's a big smurf, the smurf of all Smurf parties.
What if we smurfed some fireworks?
Me, I don't like fireworks!
Or a big parade?
Me, I don't like parades!
A dance, then? We could smurf under the paper lanterns!
Me, I don't like paper lanterns!
No fireworks! No parade! No dance! What do you want to smurf for the party then?
Me, I don't like parties.
He's in a foul smurf!
Yes! He's been like that ever since he got smurfed by the Bzz fly! (1) Some of it has stuck with him!
Hey! There's Papa Smurf! Let's ask his advice!
Hmm! Let's see... Ah! I think I have an idea!
1

(1) See THE SMURFS graphic novel #1 "The Purple Smurfs."

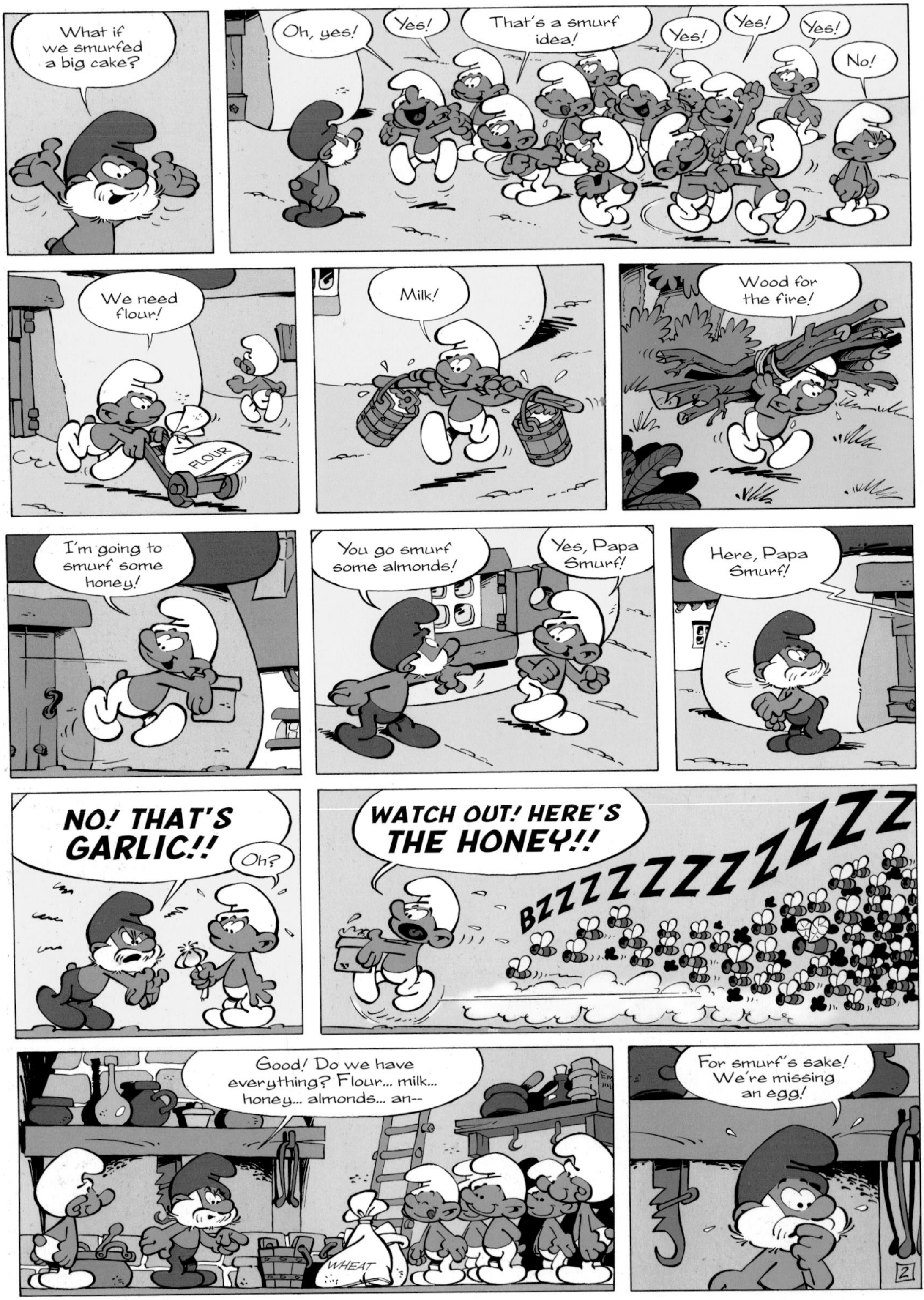

What if we smurfed a big cake?
Oh, yes!
Yes!
That's a smurf idea!
Yes!
Yes!
Yes!
No!
We need flour!
FLOUR
Milk!
Wood for the fire!
I'm going to smurf some honey!
You go smurf some almonds!
Yes, Papa Smurf!
Here, Papa Smurf!
NO! THAT'S GARLIC!!
Oh?
WATCH OUT! HERE'S THE HONEY!!
BZZZZZZZZZZZZZ
Good! Do we have everything? Flour... milk... honey... almonds... an--
WHEAT
For smurf's sake! We're missing an egg!
2

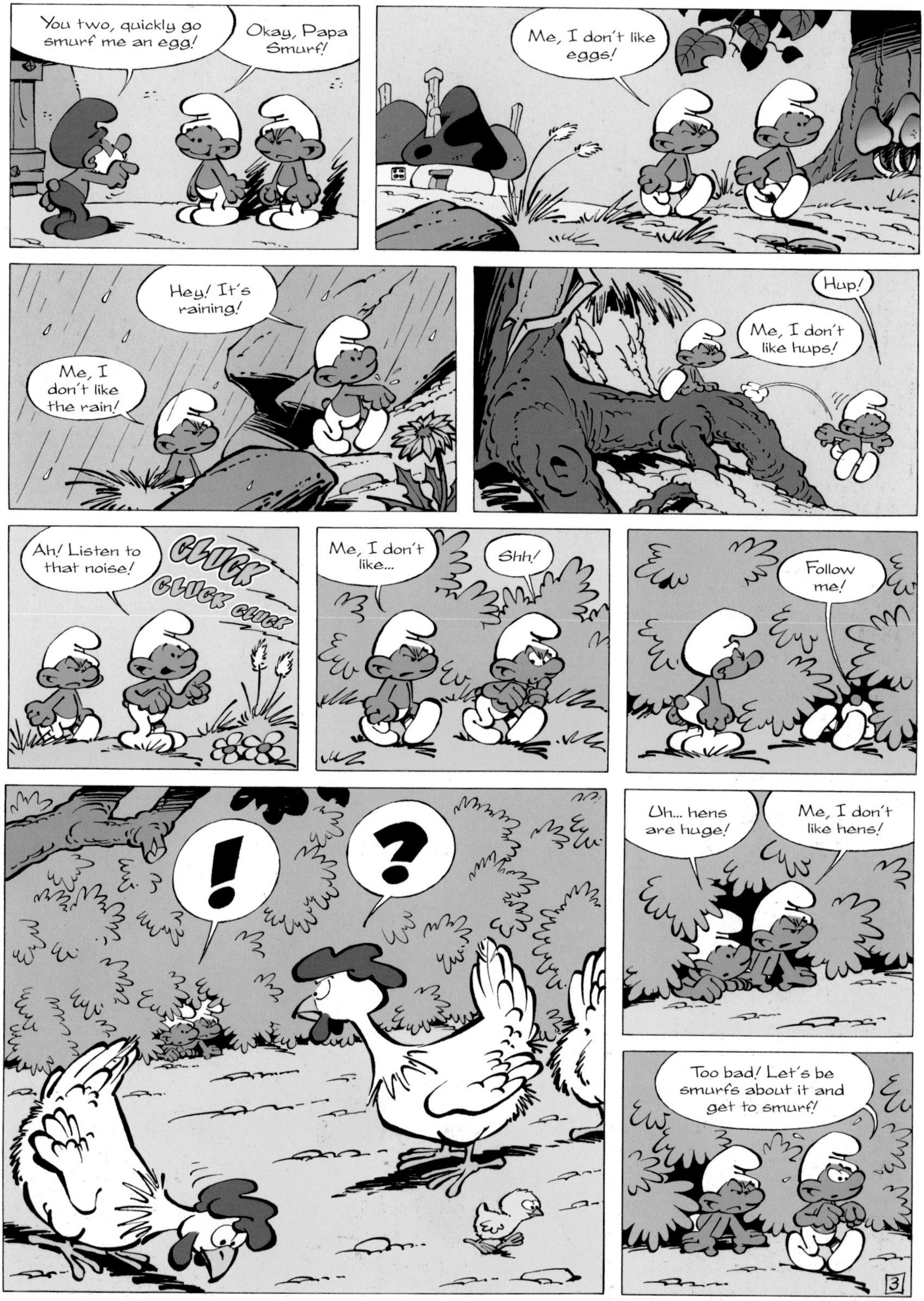
You two, quickly go smurf me an egg!
Okay, Papa Smurf!
Me, I don't like eggs!
Hey! It's raining!
Me, I don't like the rain!
Hup!
Me, I don't like hups!
Ah! Listen to that noise!
CLUCK CLUCK CLUCK CLUCK
Me, I don't like...
Shh!
Follow me!
!
?
Uh... hens are huge!
Me, I don't like hens!
Too bad! Let's be smurfs about it and get to smurf!
3

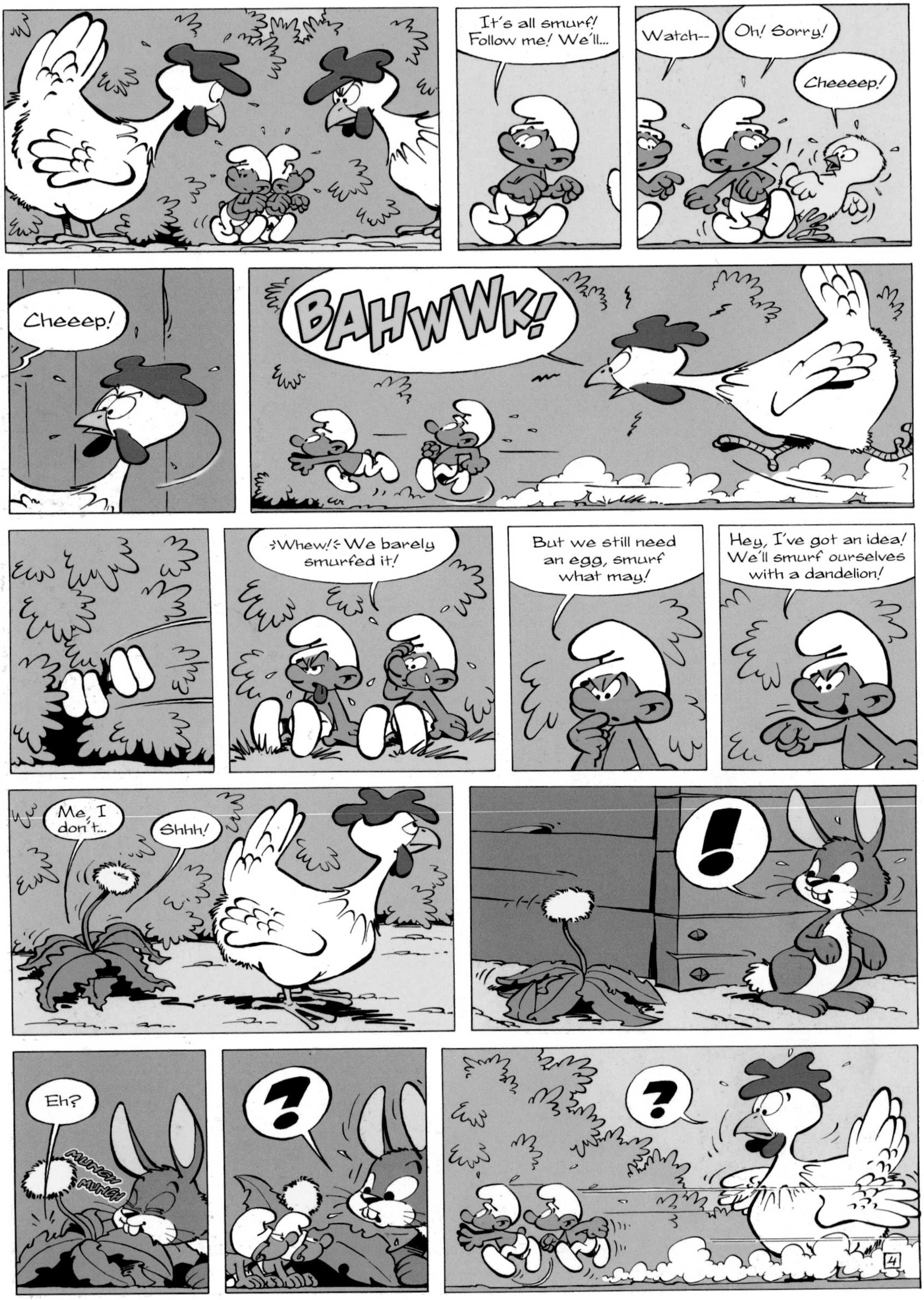

It's all smurf! Follow me! We'll...
Watch--
Oh! Sorry!
Cheeeep!
Cheeep!
BAHWWK!
Whew! We barely smurfed it!
But we still need an egg, smurf what may!
Hey, I've got an idea! We'll smurf ourselves with a dandelion!
Me, I don't...
Shhh!
!
Eh?
MUNCH MUNCH
?
?
4

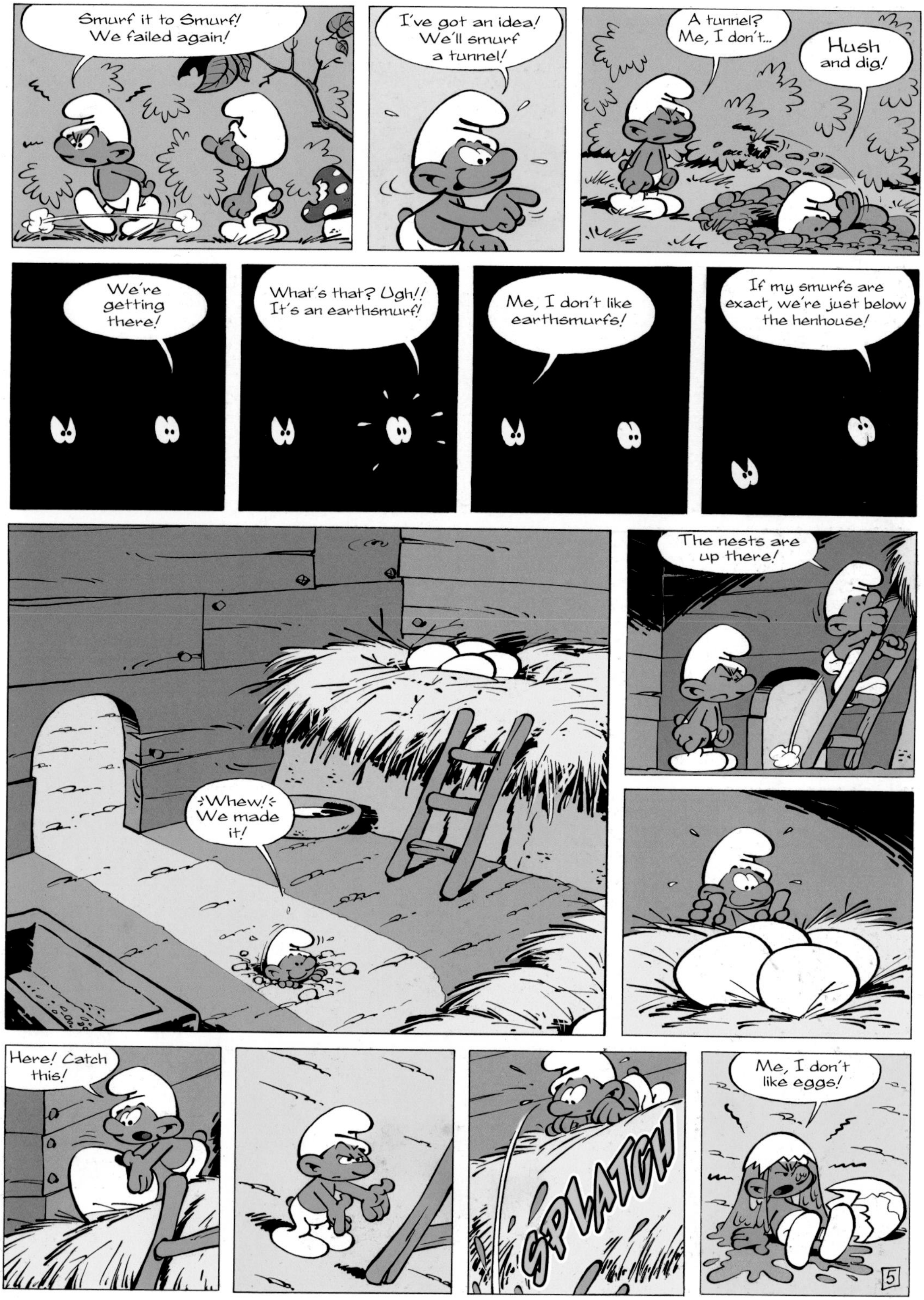
Smurf it to Smurf! We failed again!
I've got an idea! We'll smurf a tunnel!
A tunnel? Me, I don't...
Hush and dig!
We're getting there!
What's that? Ugh!! It's an earthsmurf!
Me, I don't like earthsmurfs!
If my smurfs are exact, we're just below the henhouse!
Whew! We made it!
The nests are up there!
Here! Catch this!
SPLATCH
Me, I don't like eggs!
5

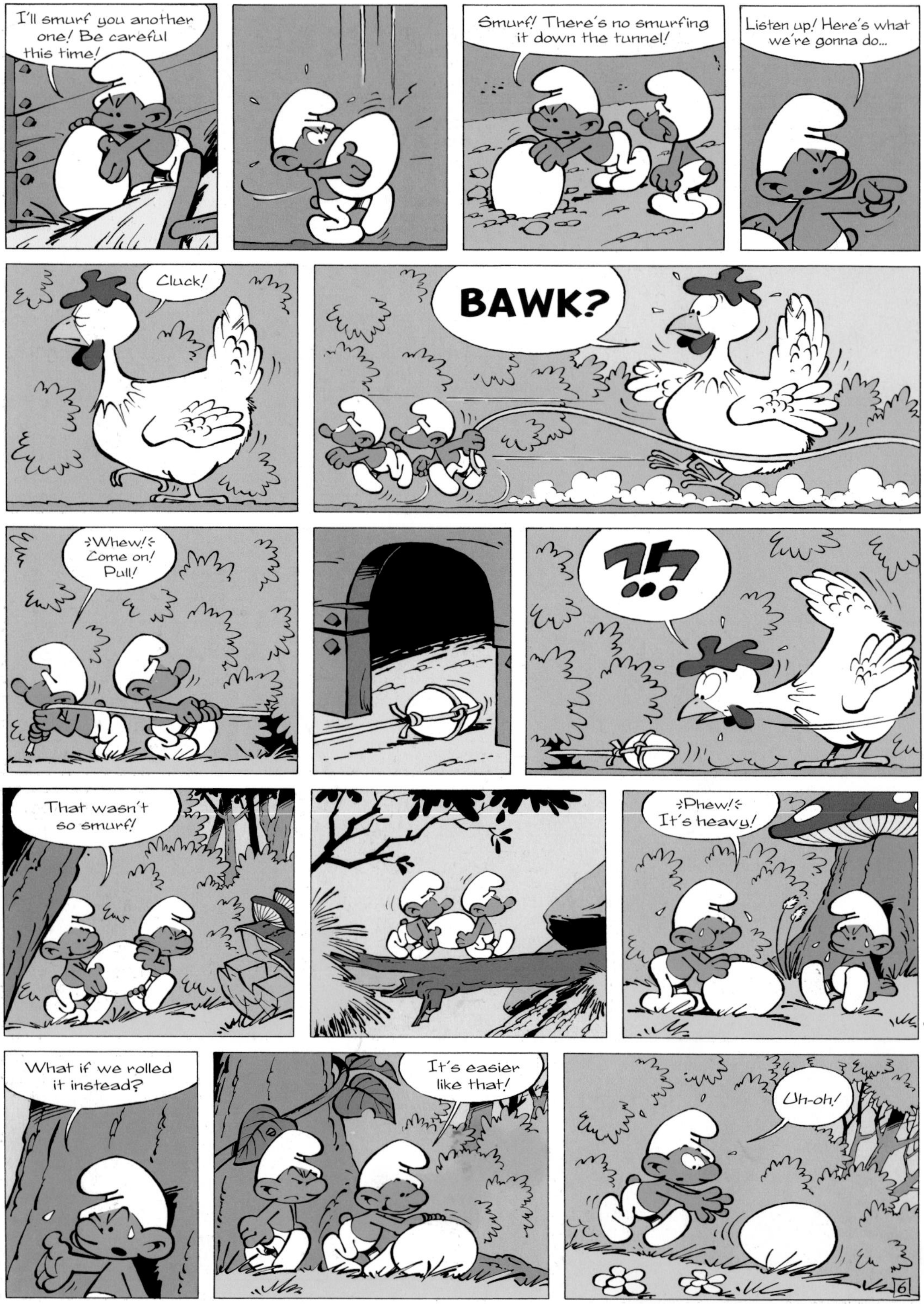
I'll smurf you another one! Be careful this time!
Smurf! There's no smurfing it down the tunnel!
Listen up! Here's what we're gonna do...
Cluck!
BAWK?
Whew! Come on! Pull!
?!...
That wasn't so smurf!
Phew! It's heavy!
What if we rolled it instead?
It's easier like that!
Uh-oh!
6

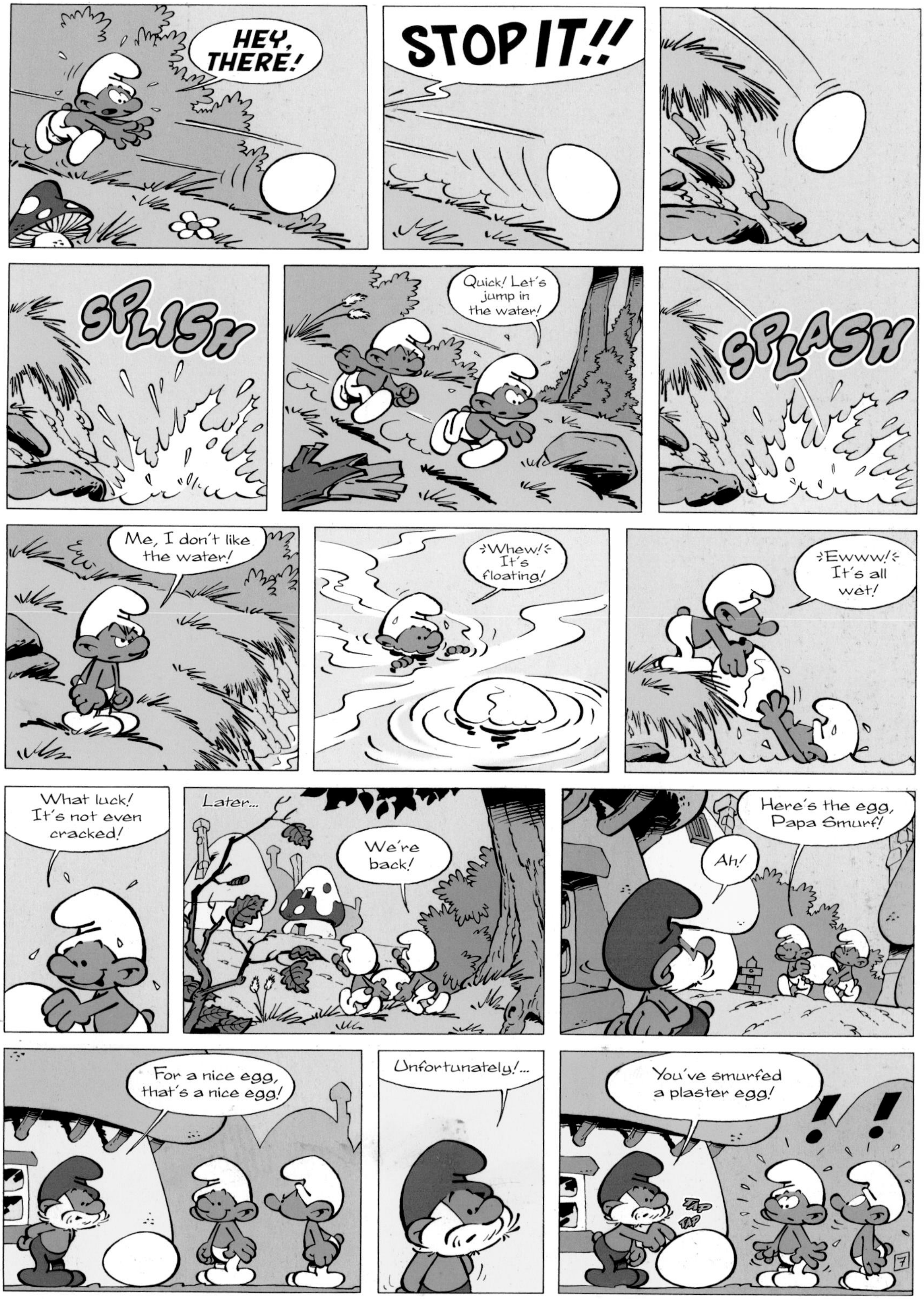
HEY, THERE!
STOP IT!!
SPLISH
Quick! Let's jump in the water!
SPLASH
Me, I don't like the water!
Whew! It's floating!
Ewww! It's all wet!
What luck! It's not even cracked!
Later...
We're back!
Here's the egg, Papa Smurf!
Ah!
For a nice egg, that's a nice egg!
Unfortunately!...
You've smurfed a plaster egg!
TAP
TAP
!!
7

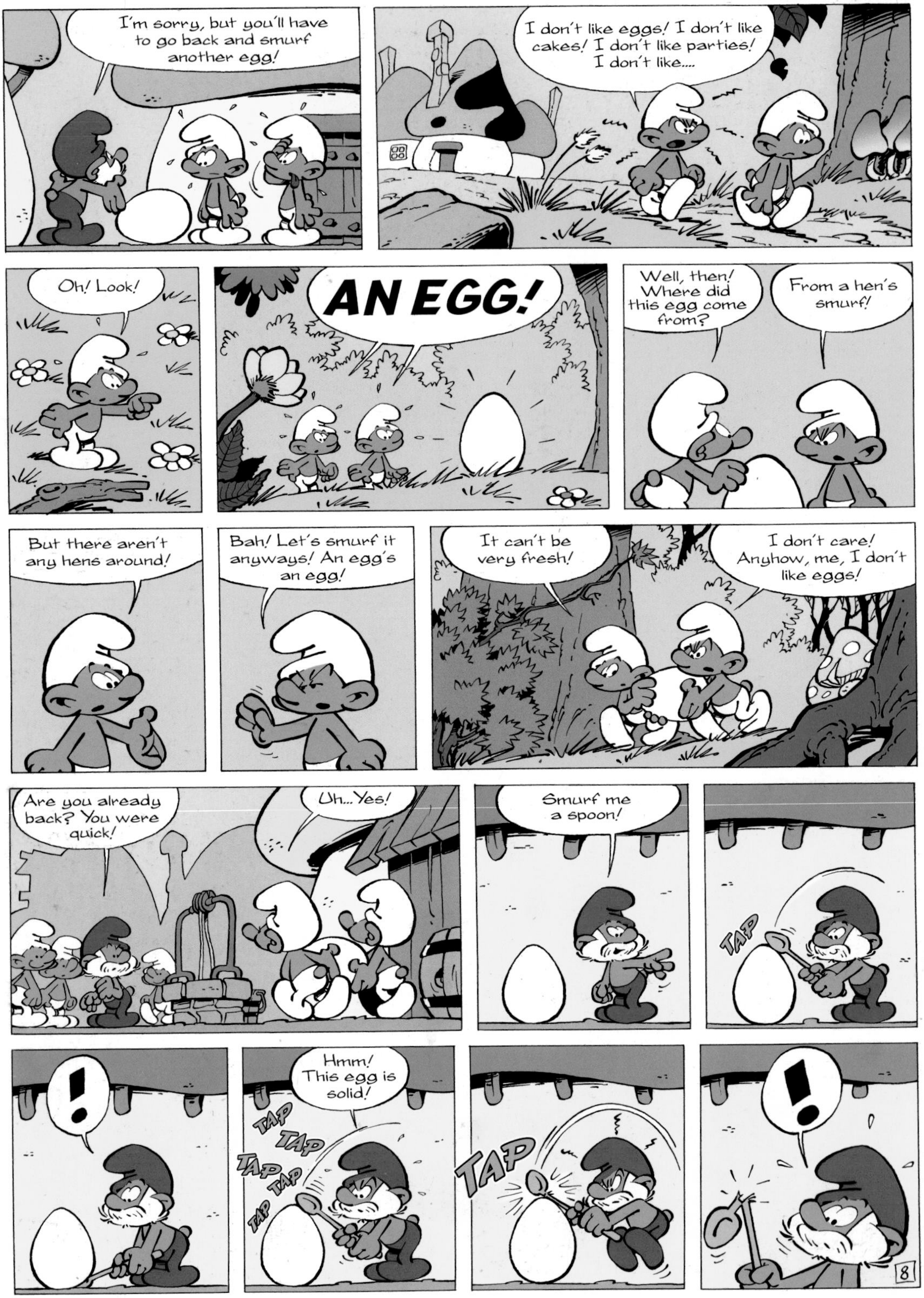
I'm sorry, but you'll have to go back and smurf another egg!
I don't like eggs! I don't like cakes! I don't like parties! I don't like....
Oh! Look!
AN EGG!
Well, then! Where did this egg come from?
From a hen's smurf!
But there aren't any hens around!
Bah! Let's smurf it anyways! An egg's an egg!
It can't be very fresh!
I don't care! Anyhow, me, I don't like eggs!
Are you already back? You were quick!
Uh... Yes!
Smurf me a spoon!
TAP
!
Hmm! This egg is solid!
TAP TAP TAP TAP TAP TAP
TAP
!
8

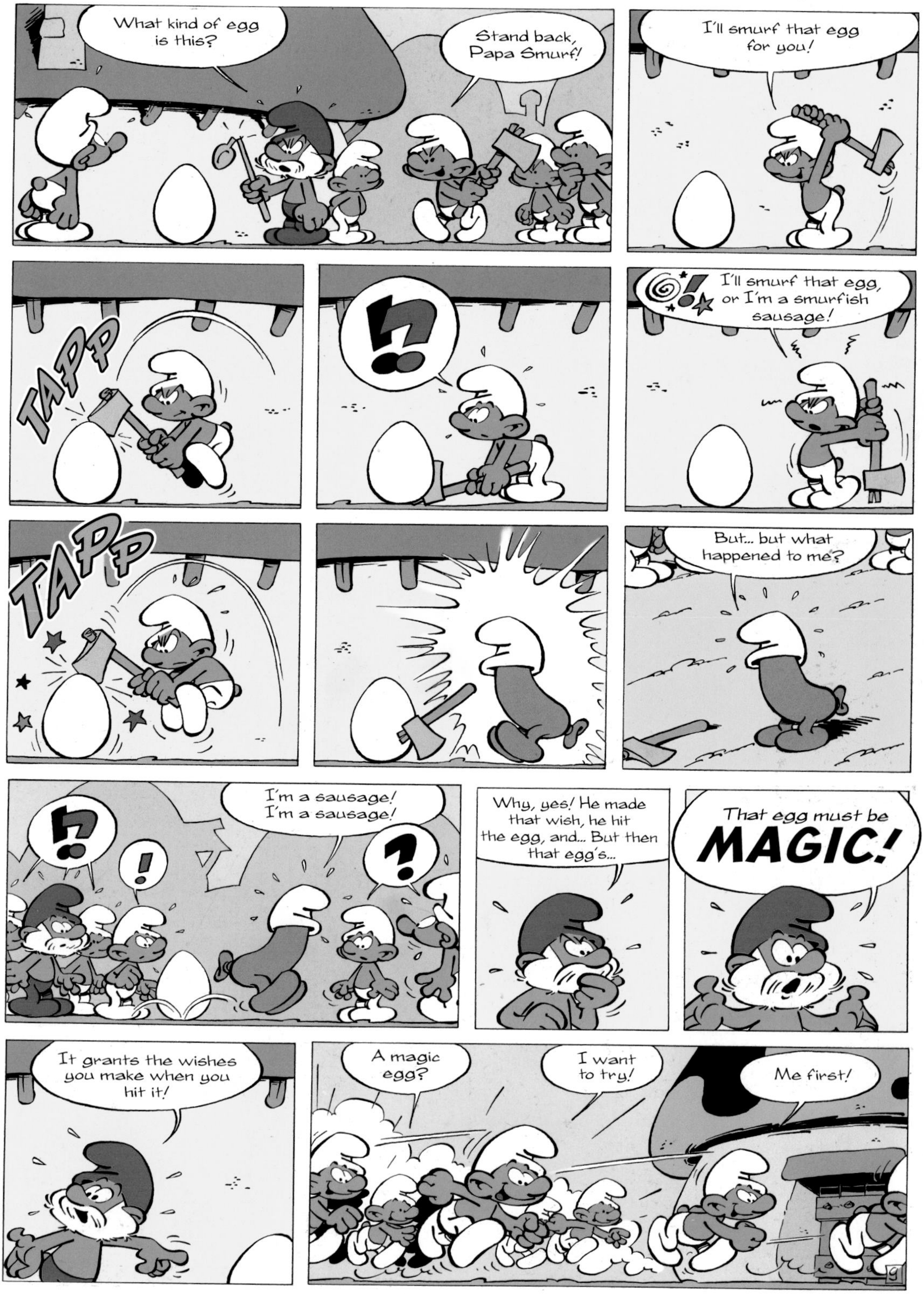

What kind of egg is this?
Stand back, Papa Smurf!
I'll smurf that egg for you!
TAPP
I'll smurf that egg, or I'm a smurfish sausage!
TAPP
But... but what happened to me?
I'm a sausage! I'm a sausage!
Why, yes! He made that wish, he hit the egg, and... But then that egg's...
That egg must be MAGIC!
It grants the wishes you make when you hit it!
A magic egg?
I want to try!
Me first!

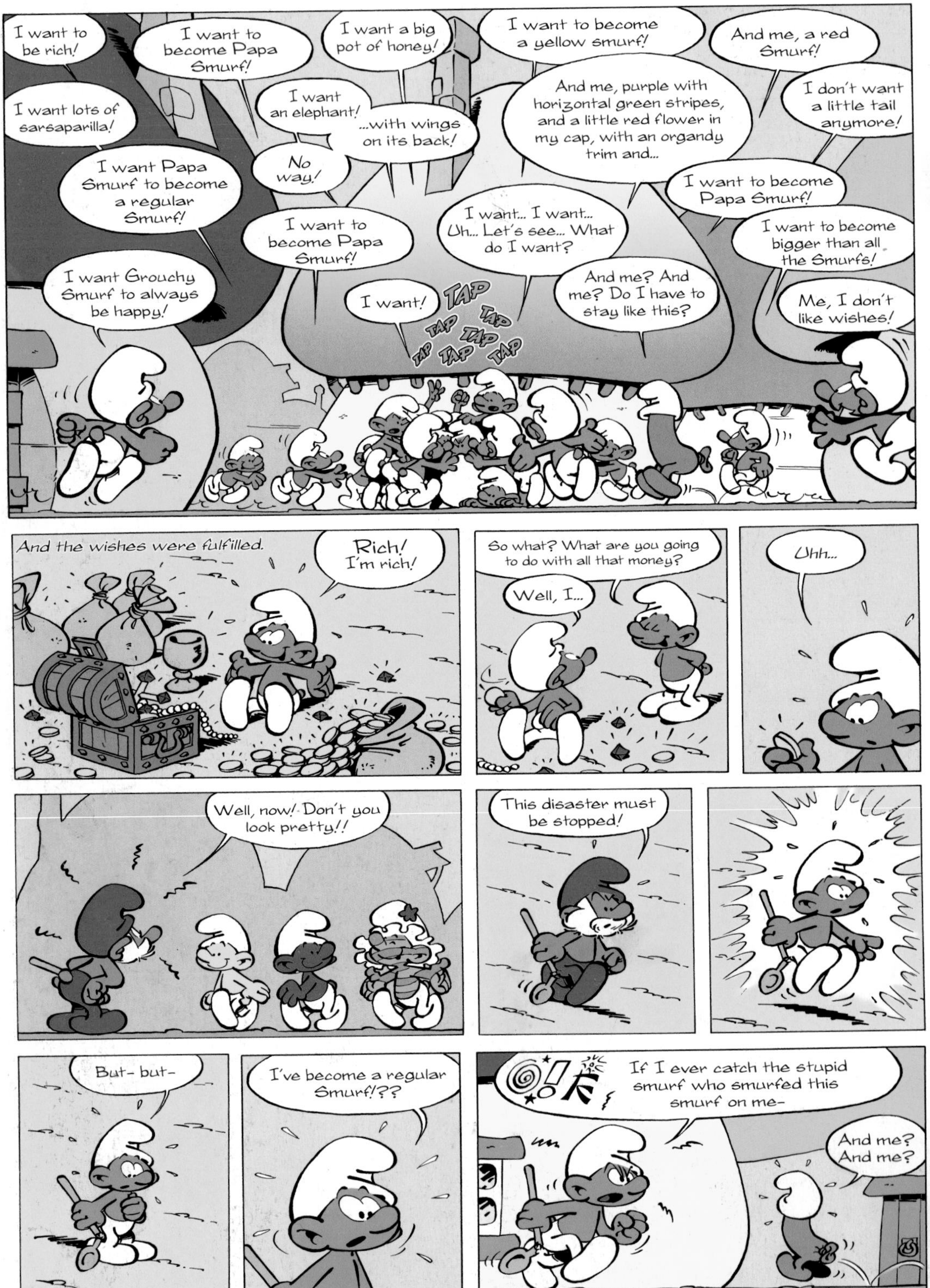
I want to be rich!
I want to become Papa Smurf!
I want a big pot of honey!
I want to become a yellow smurf!
And me, a red Smurf!
I want lots of sarsaparilla!
I want an elephant!
...with wings on its back!
No way!
And me, purple with horizontal green stripes, and a little red flower in my cap, with an organdy trim and...
I don't want a little tail anymore!
I want Papa Smurf to become a regular Smurf!
I want to become Papa Smurf!
I want to become Papa Smurf!
I want... I want... Uh... Let's see... What do I want?
I want to become bigger than all the Smurfs!
I want Grouchy Smurf to always be happy!
I want!
TAP TAP TAP TAP TAP TAP TAP
And me? And me? Do I have to stay like this?
Me, I don't like wishes!
And the wishes were fulfilled.
Rich! I'm rich!
So what? What are you going to do with all that money?
Well, I...
Uhh...
Well, now! Don't you look pretty!!
This disaster must be stopped!
But- but-
I've become a regular Smurf!??
If I ever catch the stupid smurf who smurfed this smurf on me-
And me? And me?

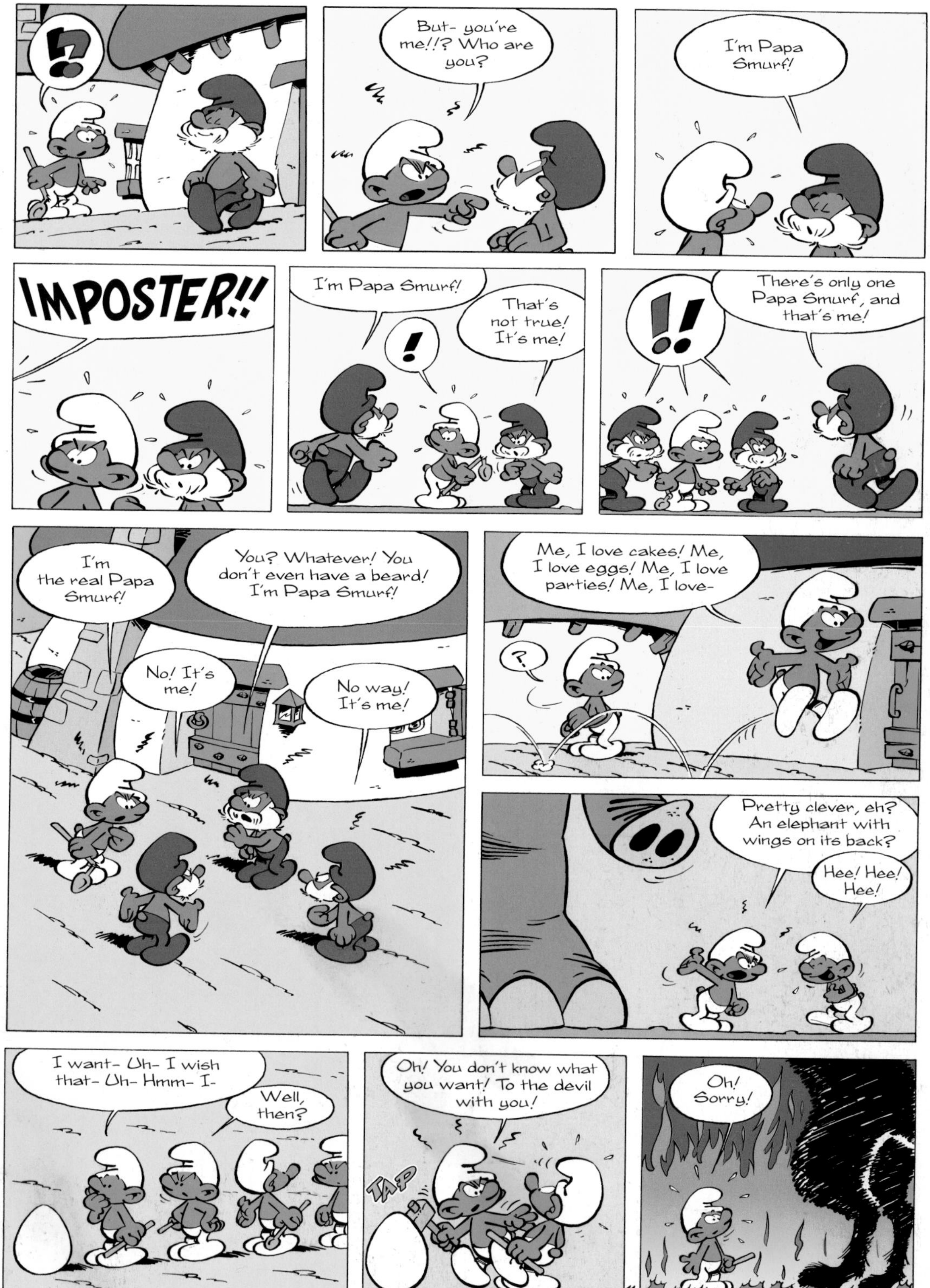

!?
But- you're me!!? Who are you?
I'm Papa Smurf!
IMPOSTER!!
I'm Papa Smurf!
!
That's not true! It's me!
!!
There's only one Papa Smurf, and that's me!
I'm the real Papa Smurf!
You? Whatever! You don't even have a beard! I'm Papa Smurf!
No! It's me!
No way! It's me!
Me, I love cakes! Me, I love eggs! Me, I love parties! Me, I love-
?
Pretty clever, eh? An elephant with wings on its back?
Hee! Hee! Hee!
I want- Uh- I wish that- Uh- Hmm- I-
Well, then?
Oh! You don't know what you want! To the devil with you!
TAP
Oh! Sorry!

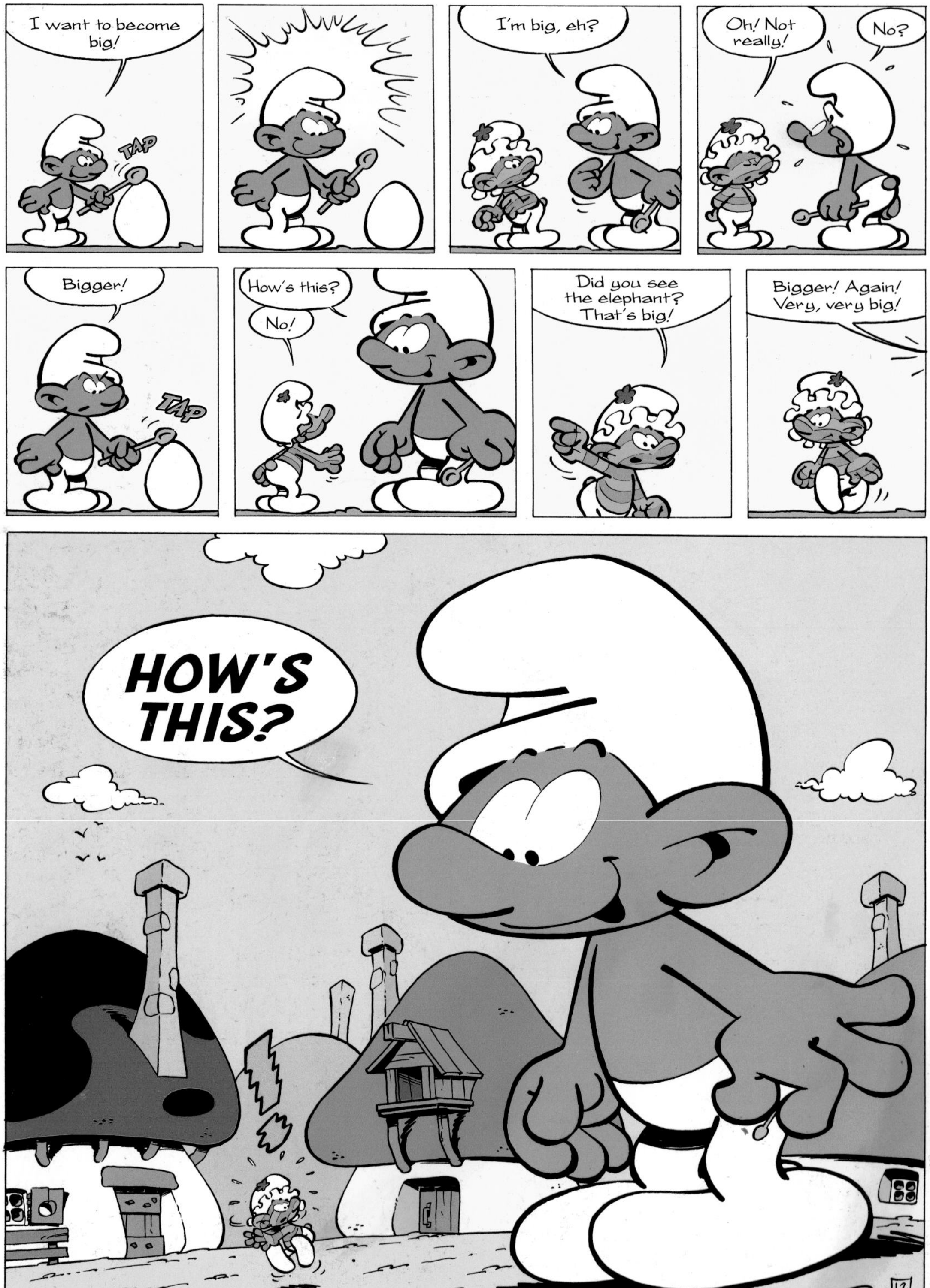
I want to become big!
TAP
I'm big, eh?
Oh! Not really!
No?
Bigger!
TAP
How's this?
No!
Did you see the elephant? That's big!
Bigger! Again! Very, very big!
HOW'S THIS?
12

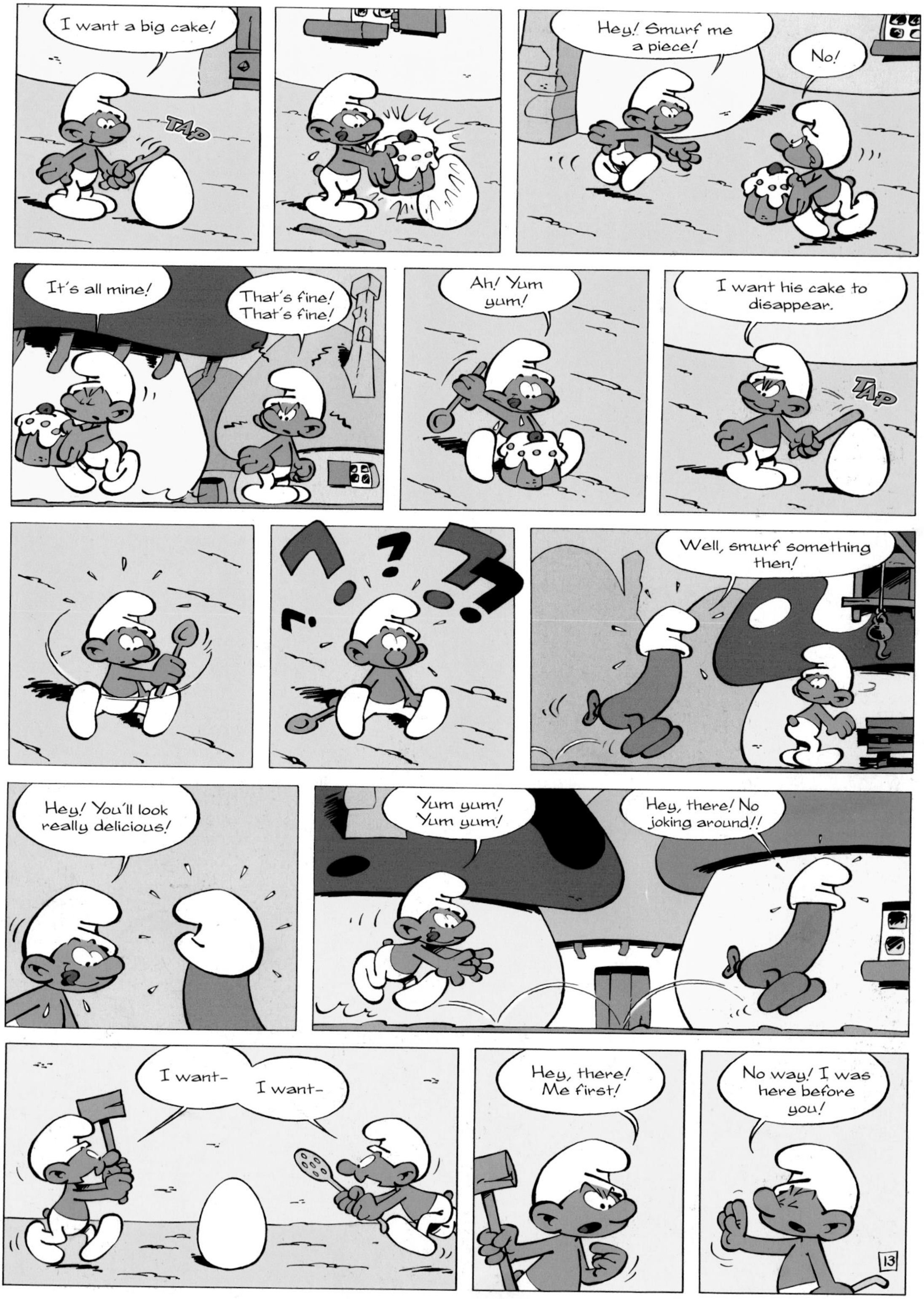
I want a big cake!
TAP
Hey! Smurf me a piece!
No!
It's all mine!
That's fine! That's fine!
Ah! Yum yum!
I want his cake to disappear.
TAP
Well, smurf something then!
Hey! You'll look really delicious!
Yum yum! Yum yum!
Hey, there! No joking around!!
I want-
I want-
Hey, there! Me first!
No way! I was here before you!
13

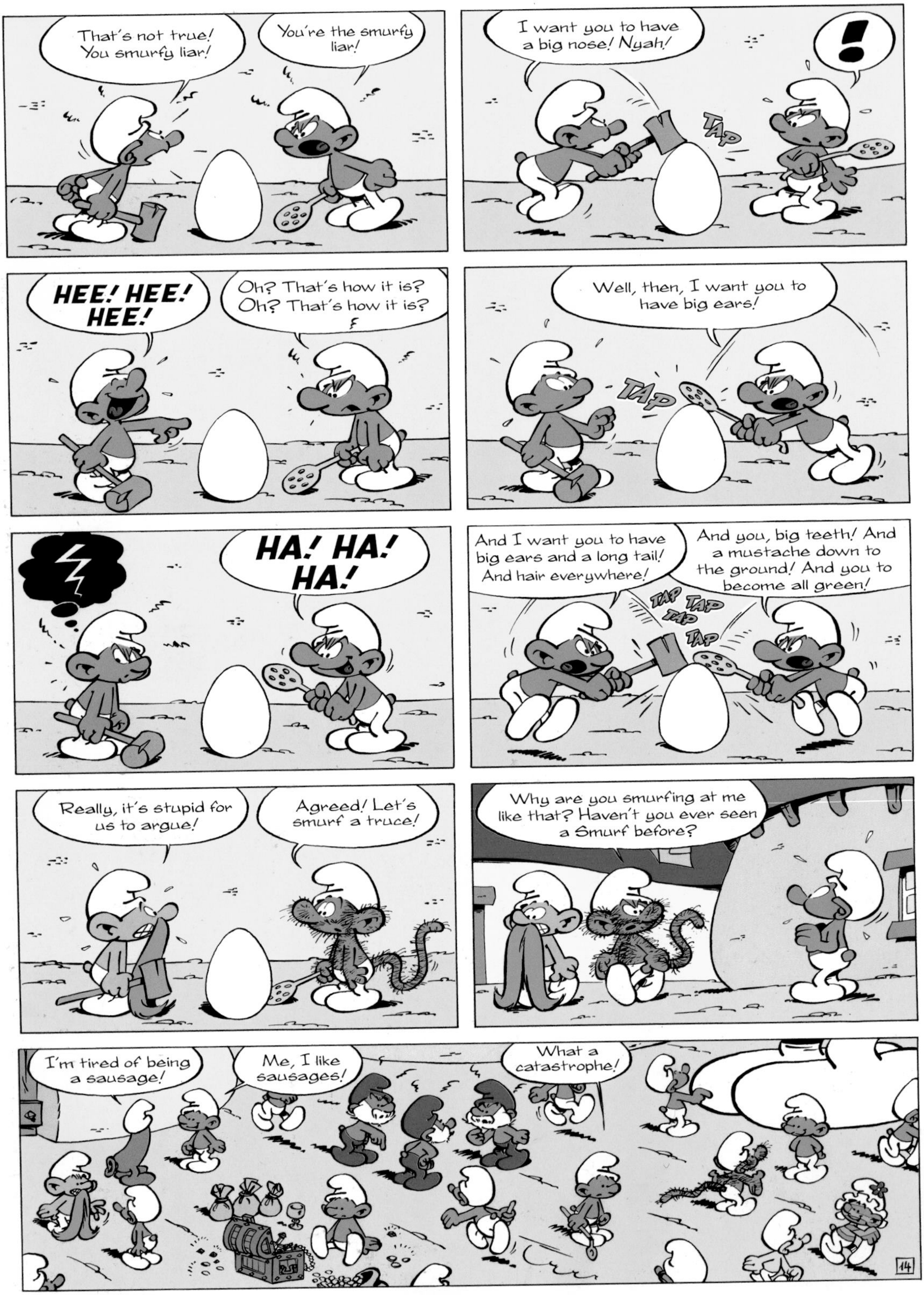
That's not true! You smurfy liar!
You're the smurfy liar!
I want you to have a big nose! Nyah!
TAP
!
HEE! HEE! HEE!
Oh? That's how it is? Oh? That's how it is?
Well, then, I want you to have big ears!
TAP
HA! HA! HA!
And I want you to have big ears and a long tail! And hair everywhere!
And you, big teeth! And a mustache down to the ground! And you to become all green!
TAP TAP TAP TAP
Really, it's stupid for us to argue!
Agreed! Let's smurf a truce!
Why are you smurfing at me like that? Haven't you ever seen a Smurf before?
I'm tired of being a sausage!
Me, I like sausages!
What a catastrophe!
14

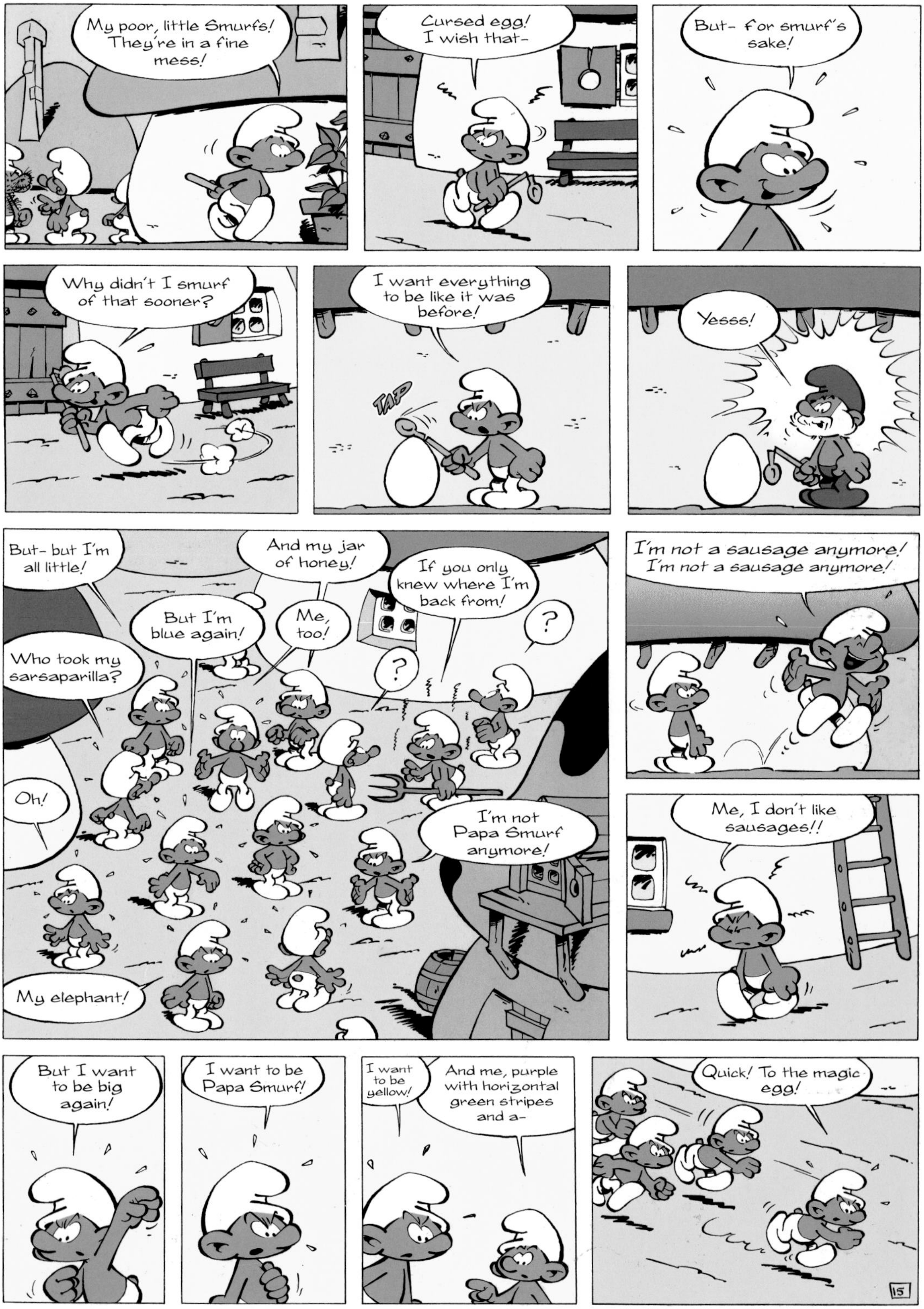

My poor, little Smurfs! They're in a fine mess!
Cursed egg! I wish that-
But- for smurf's sake!
Why didn't I smurf of that sooner?
I want everything to be like it was before!
TAP
Yesss!
But- but I'm all little!
And my jar of honey!
If you only knew where I'm back from!
But I'm blue again!
Me, too!
?
?
Who took my sarsaparilla?
Oh!
I'm not Papa Smurf anymore!
My elephant!
I'm not a sausage anymore! I'm not a sausage anymore!
Me, I don't like sausages!!
But I want to be big again!
I want to be Papa Smurf!
I want to be yellow!
And me, purple with horizontal green stripes and a-
Quick! To the magic egg!
15

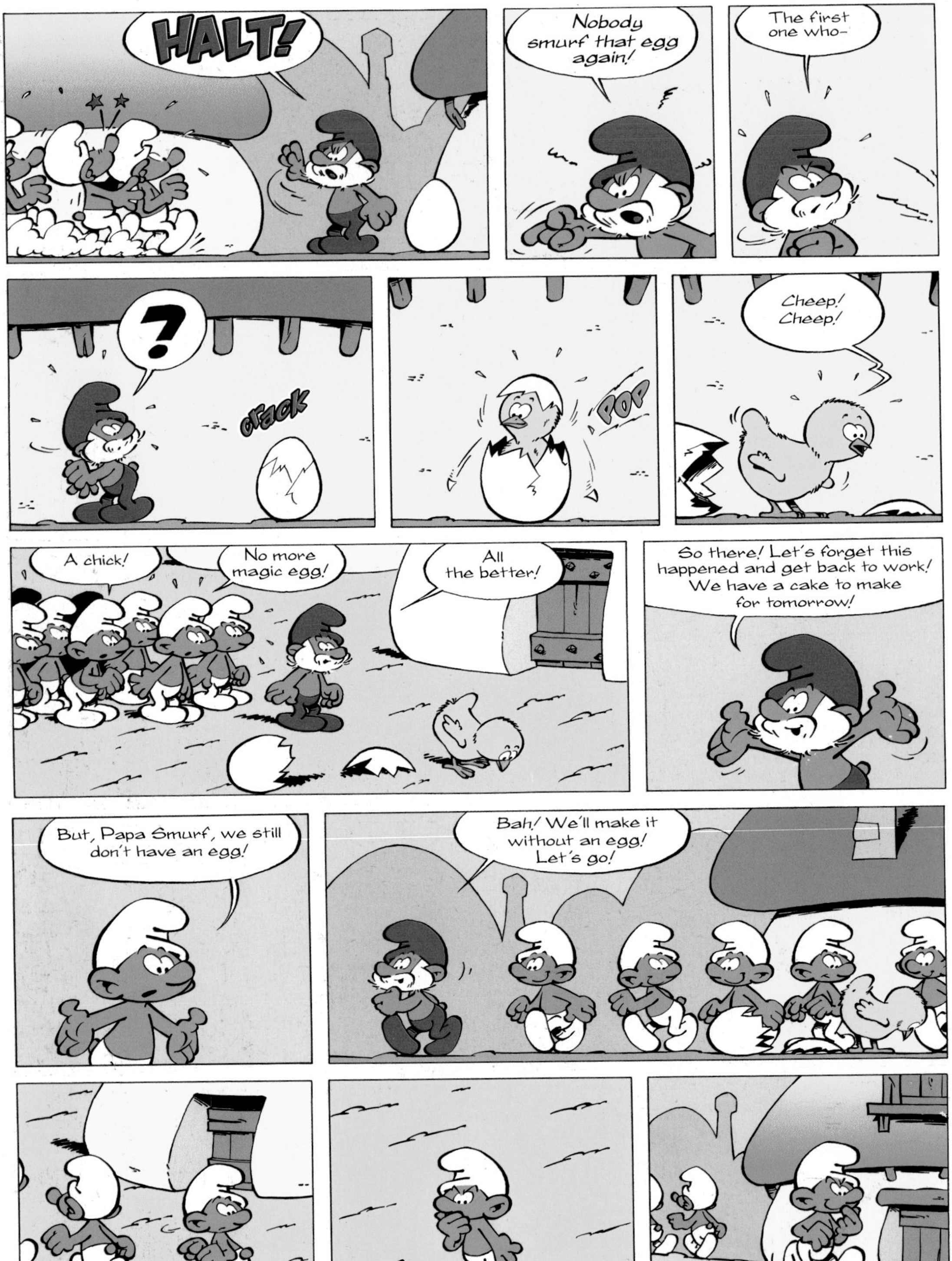
HALT!
Nobody smurf that egg again!
The first one who-
?
CRACK
POP
Cheep! Cheep!
A chick!
No more magic egg!
All the better!
So there! Let's forget this happened and get back to work! We have a cake to make for tomorrow!
But, Papa Smurf, we still don't have an egg!
Bah! We'll make it without an egg! Let's go!
16

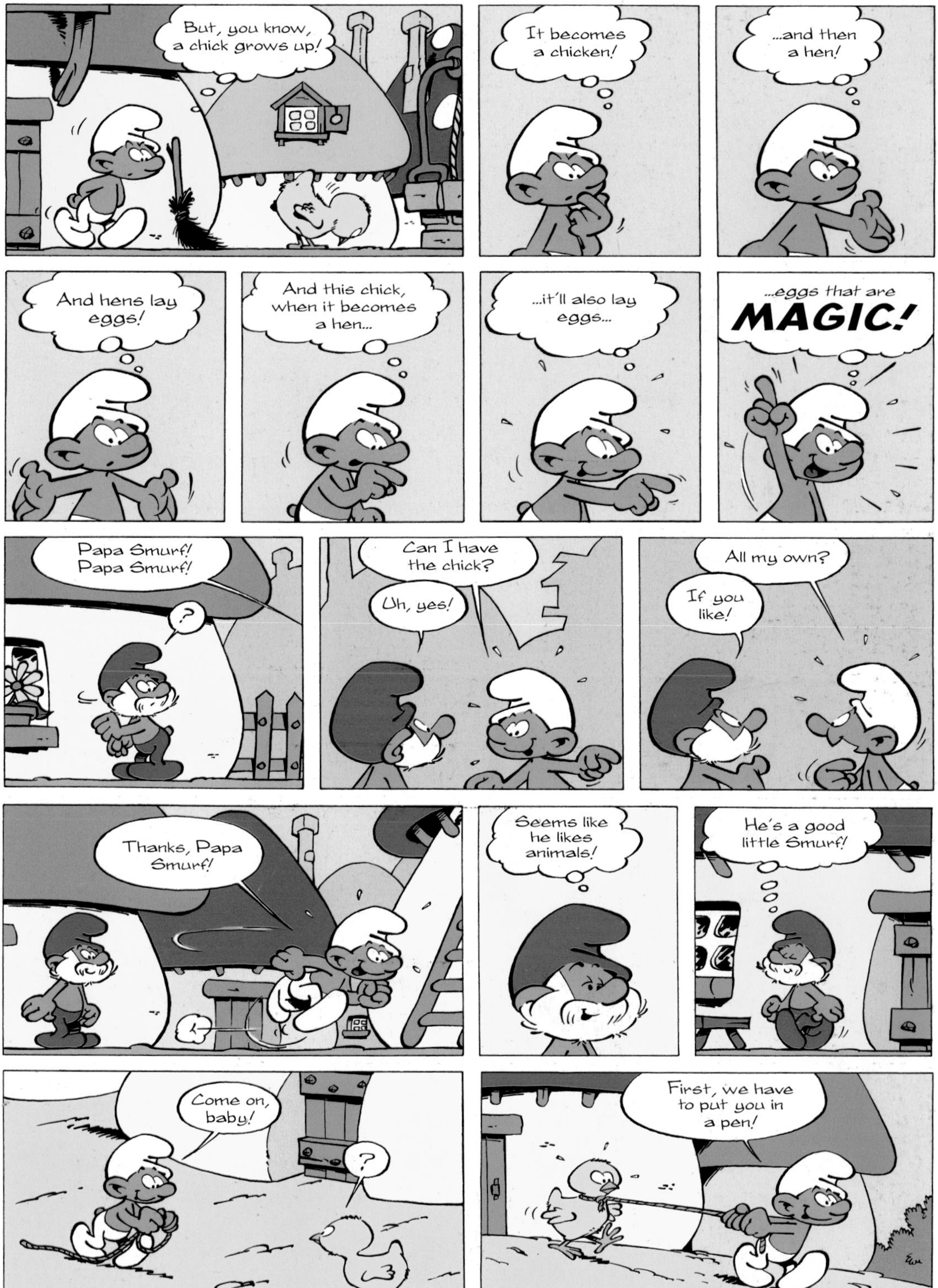

But, you know, a chick grows up!
It becomes a chicken!
...and then a hen!
And hens lay eggs!
And this chick, when it becomes a hen...
...it'll also lay eggs...
...eggs that are MAGIC!
Papa Smurf! Papa Smurf!
?
Can I have the chick?
Uh, yes!
All my own?
If you like!
Thanks, Papa Smurf!
Seems like he likes animals!
He's a good little Smurf!
Come on, baby!
?
First, we have to put you in a pen!
17

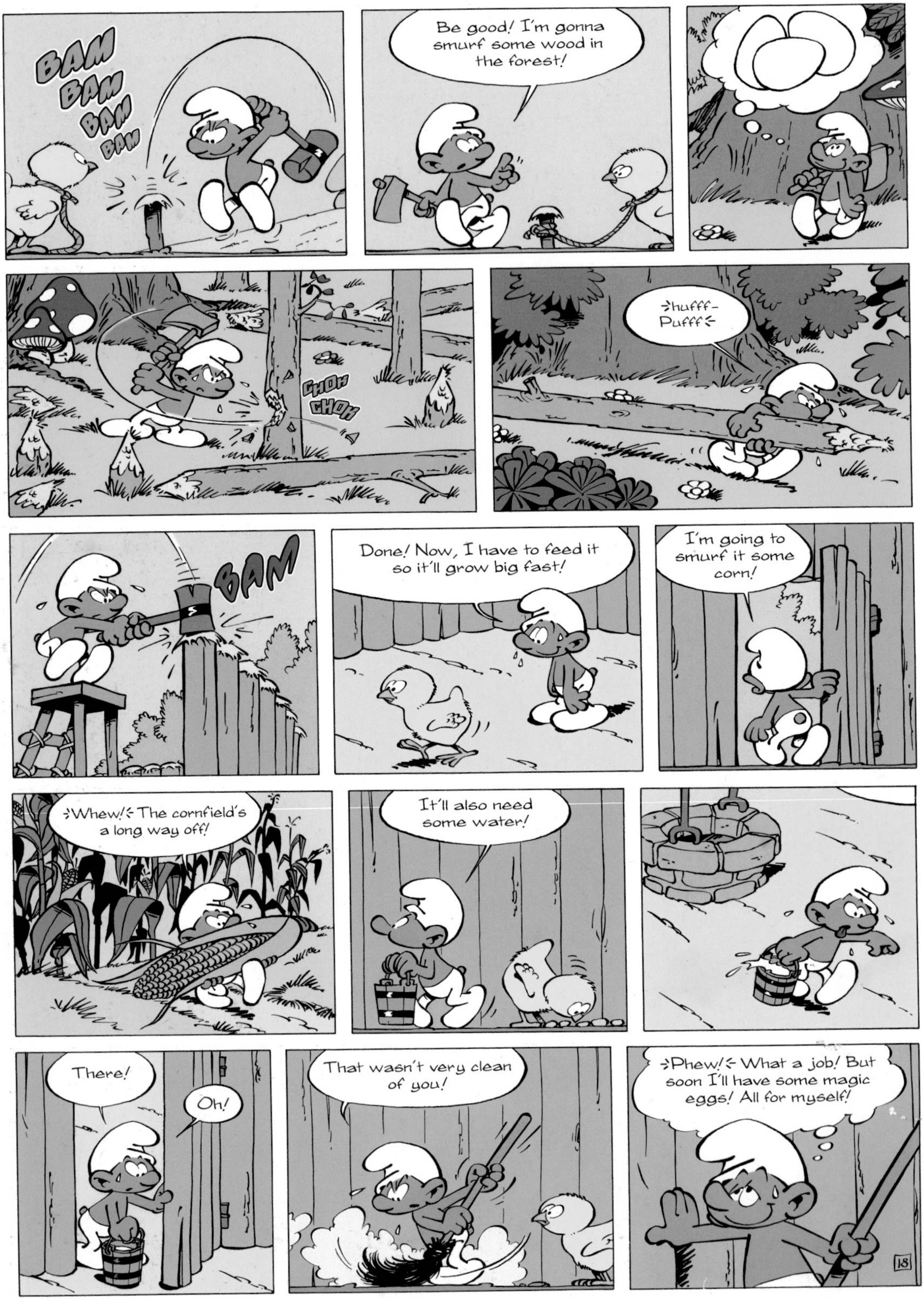
BAM BAM BAM BAM
Be good! I'm gonna smurf some wood in the forest!
CHOK CHOK
-huffff- Pufff-
BAM
Done! Now, I have to feed it so it'll grow big fast!
I'm going to smurf it some corn!
-Whew!- The cornfield's a long way off!
It'll also need some water!
There!
Oh!
That wasn't very clean of you!
-Phew!- What a job! But soon I'll have some magic eggs! All for myself!
18

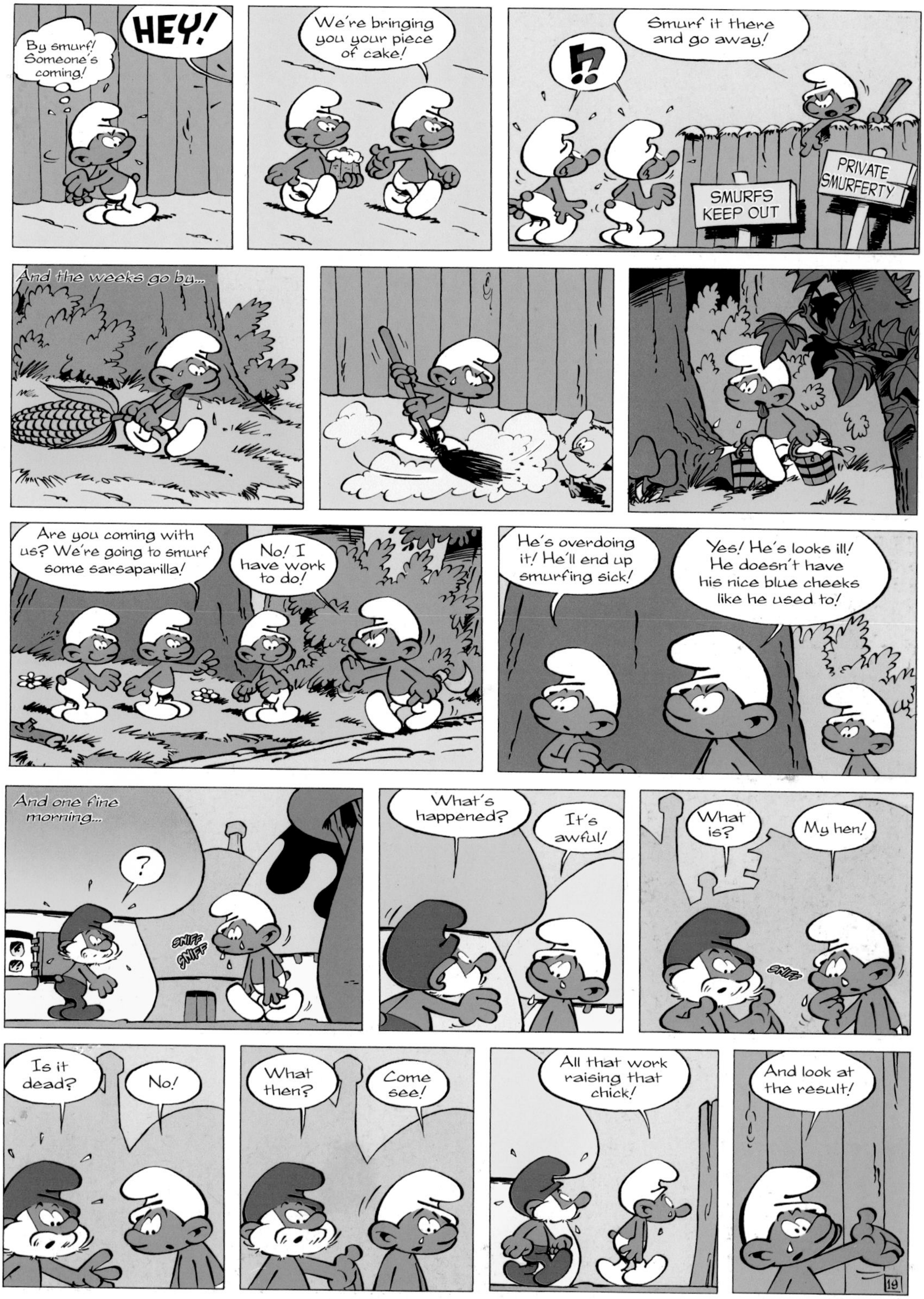

By smurf! Someone's coming!
HEY!
We're bringing you your piece of cake!
?!
Smurf it there and go away!
SMURFS KEEP OUT
PRIVATE SMURFERTY
And the weeks go by...
Are you coming with us? We're going to smurf some sarsaparilla!
No! I have work to do!
He's overdoing it! He'll end up smurfing sick!
Yes! He's looks ill! He doesn't have his nice blue cheeks like he used to!
And one fine morning...
?
SNIFF SNIFF
What's happened?
It's awful!
What is?
My hen!
SNIFF
Is it dead?
No!
What then?
Come see!
All that work raising that chick!
And look at the result!
19

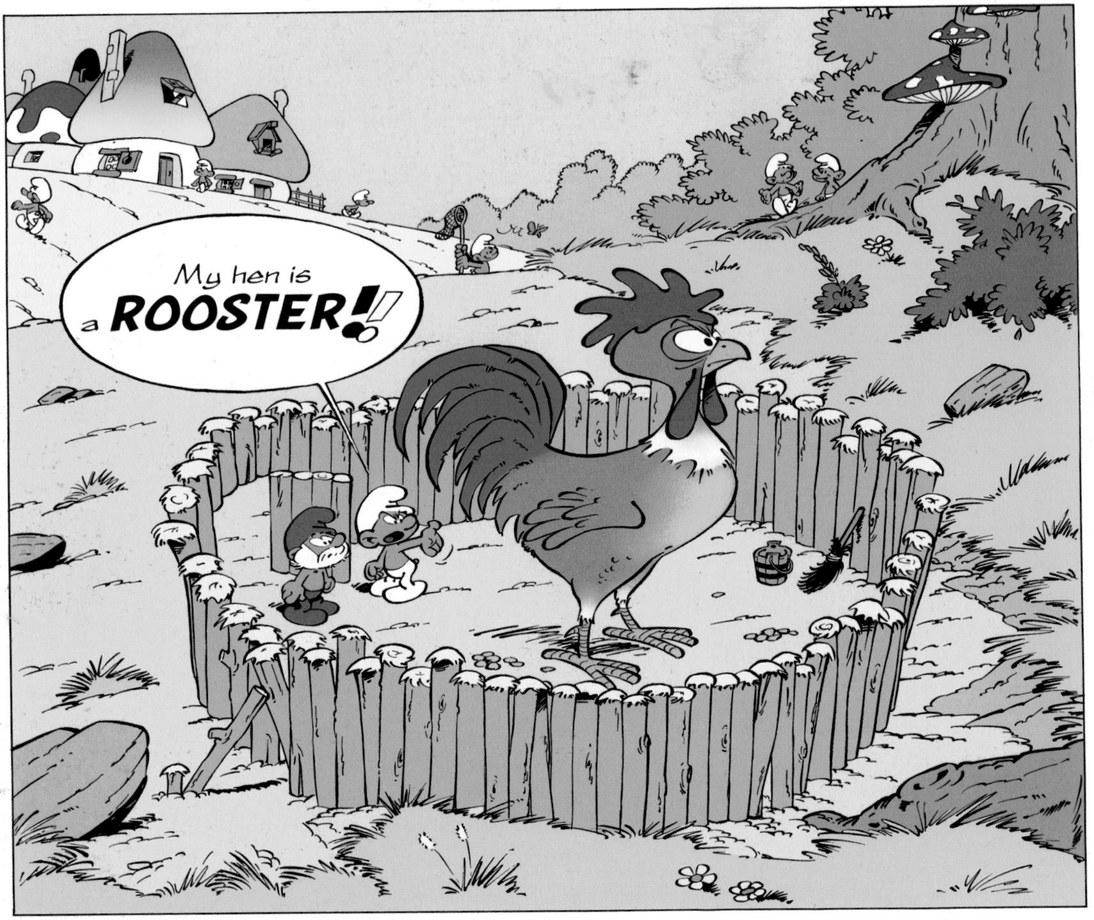
My hen is a ROOSTER!!

THE END

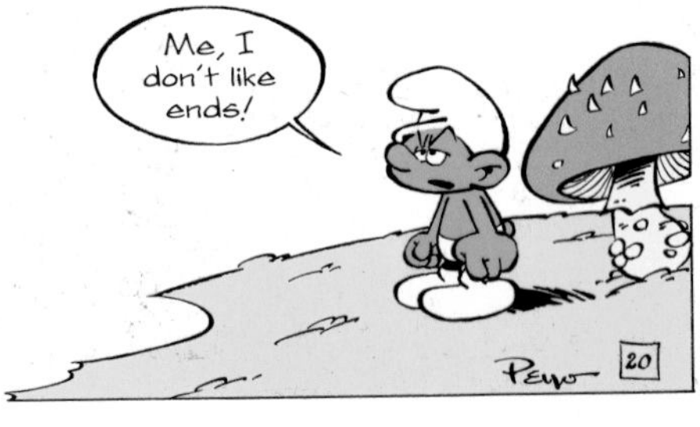
Me, I don't like ends!
PEYO
20

THE FAKE SMURF

by Peyo

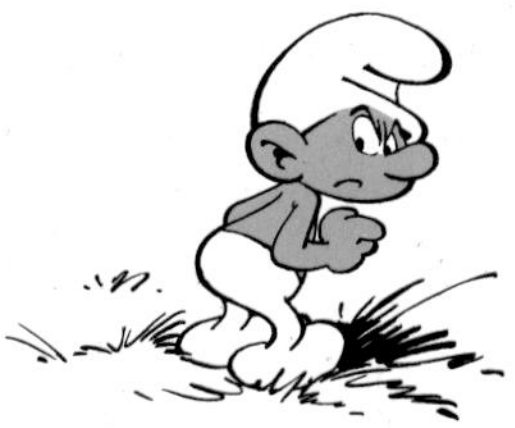

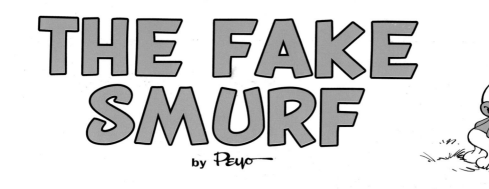

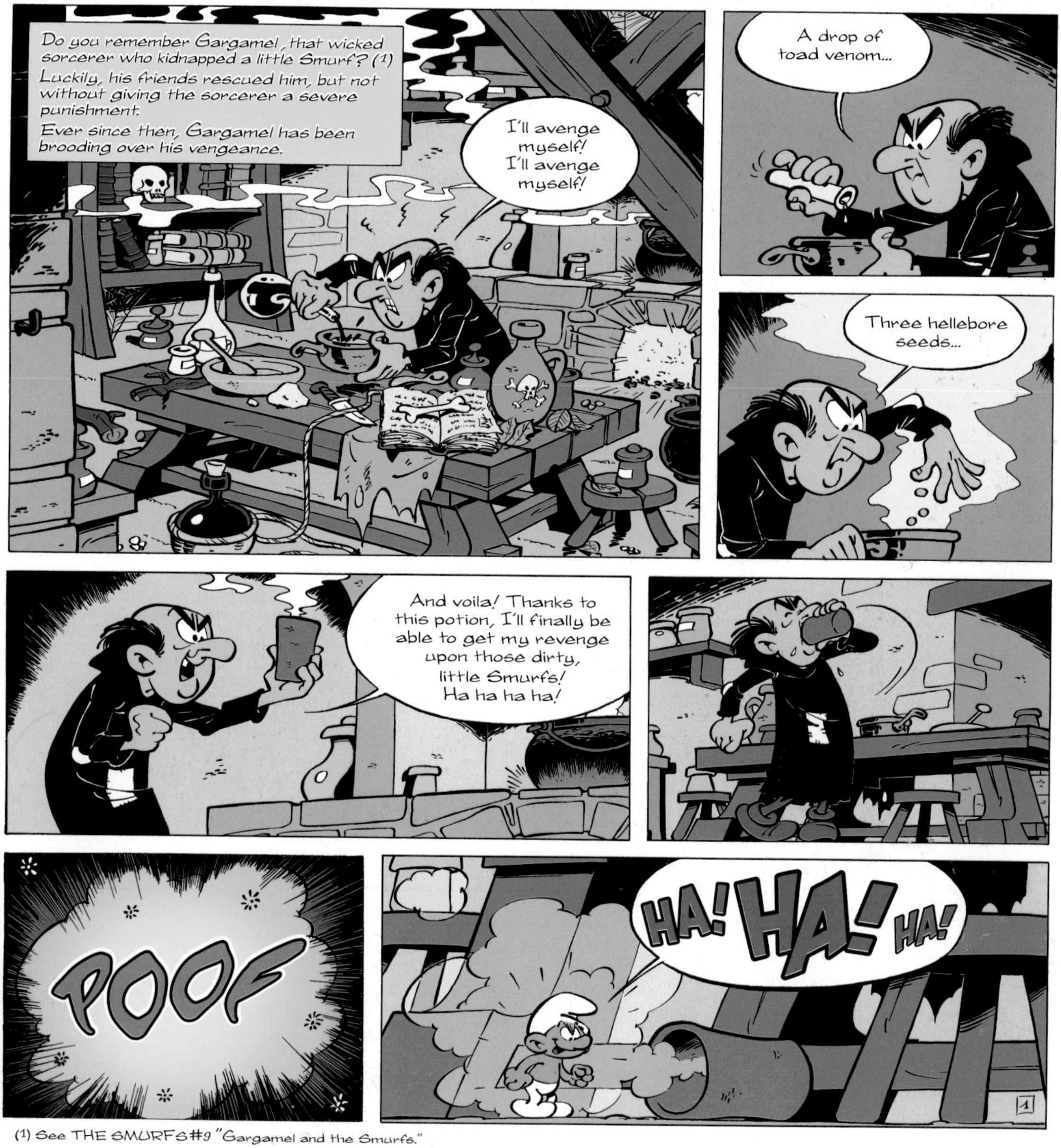
Do you remember Gargamel, that wicked sorcerer who kidnapped a little Smurf? (1)
Luckily, his friends rescued him, but not without giving the sorcerer a severe punishment.
Ever since then, Gargamel has been brooding over his vengeance.
I'll avenge myself! I'll avenge myself!
A drop of toad venom...
Three hellebore seeds...
And voila! Thanks to this potion, I'll finally be able to get my revenge upon those dirty, little Smurfs! Ha ha ha ha!
POOF
HA! HA! HA!
1

(1) See THE SMURFS #9 "Gargamel and the Smurfs."

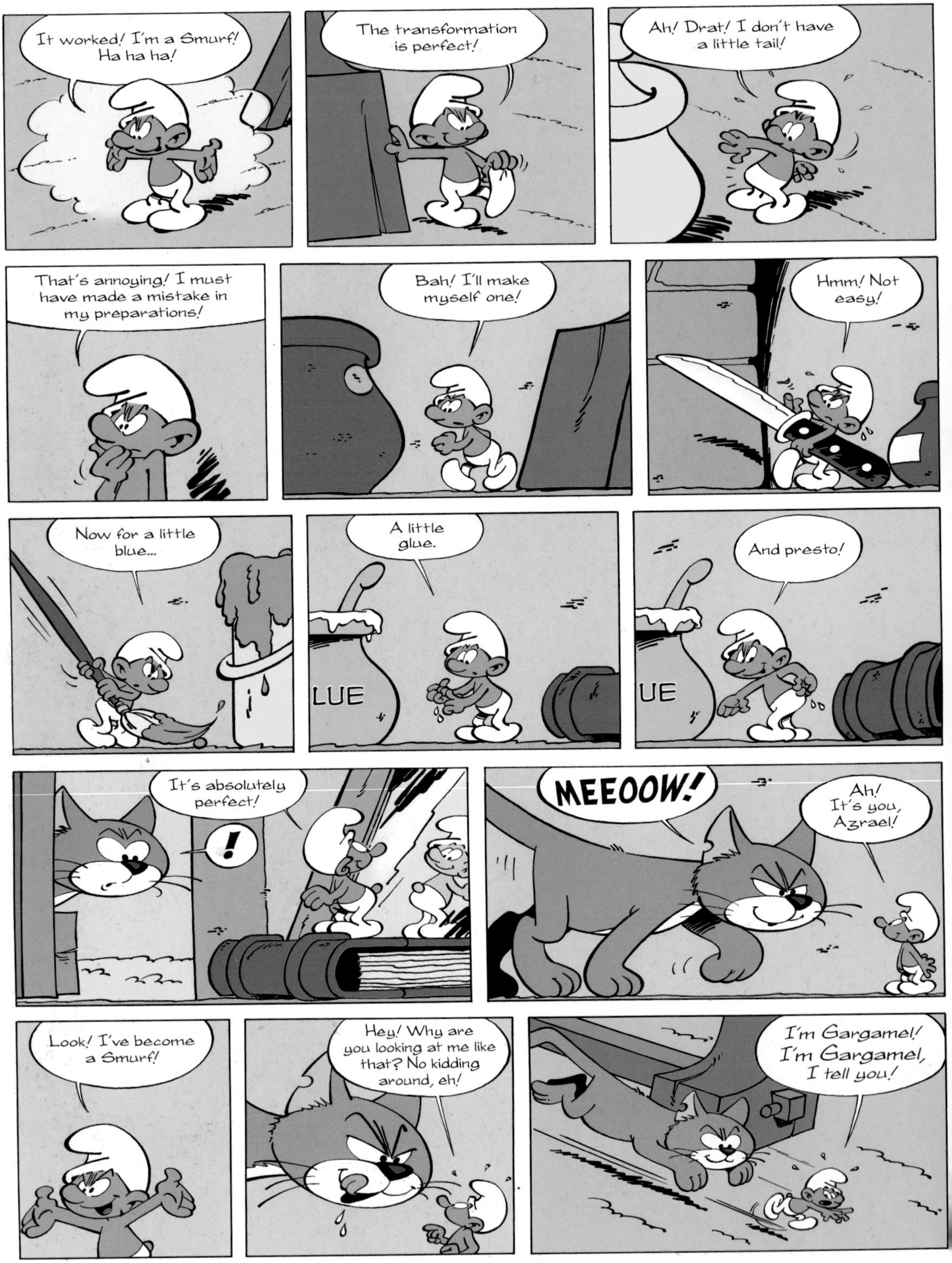
It worked! I'm a Smurf! Ha ha ha!
The transformation is perfect!
Ah! Drat! I don't have a little tail!
That's annoying! I must have made a mistake in my preparations!
Bah! I'll make myself one!
Hmm! Not easy!
Now for a little blue...
A little glue.
LUE
And presto!
UE
It's absolutely perfect!
!
MEEOOW!
Ah! It's you, Azrael!
Look! I've become a Smurf!
Hey! Why are you looking at me like that? No kidding around, eh!
I'm Gargamel! I'm Gargamel, I tell you!

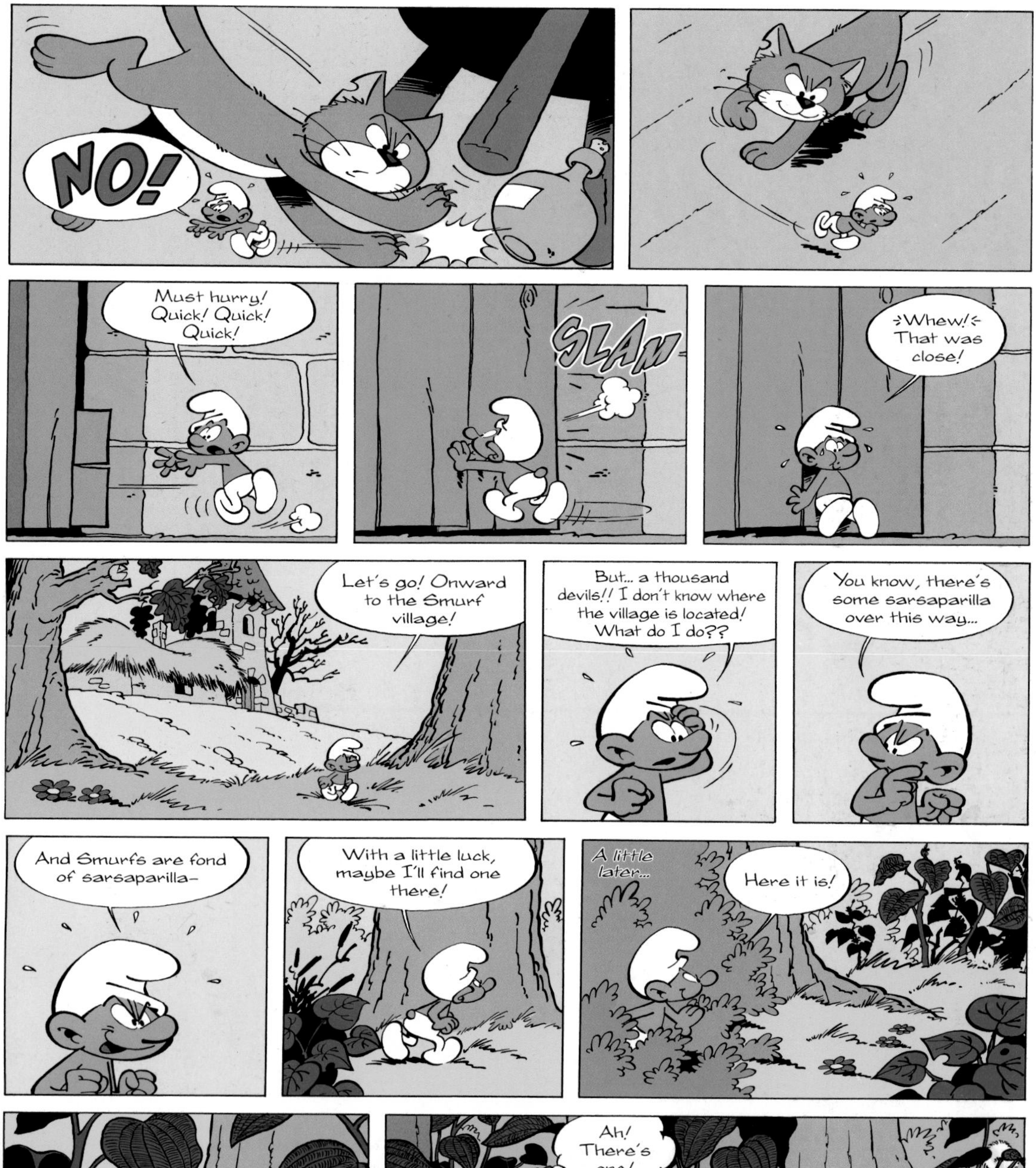
NO!
Must hurry! Quick! Quick! Quick!
SLAM
Whew! That was close!
Let's go! Onward to the Smurf village!
But... a thousand devils!! I don't know where the village is located! What do I do??
You know, there's some sarsaparilla over this way...
And Smurfs are fond of sarsaparilla-
With a little luck, maybe I'll find one there!
A little later...
Here it is!
Ah! There's one!
MUNCH CRUNCH
3

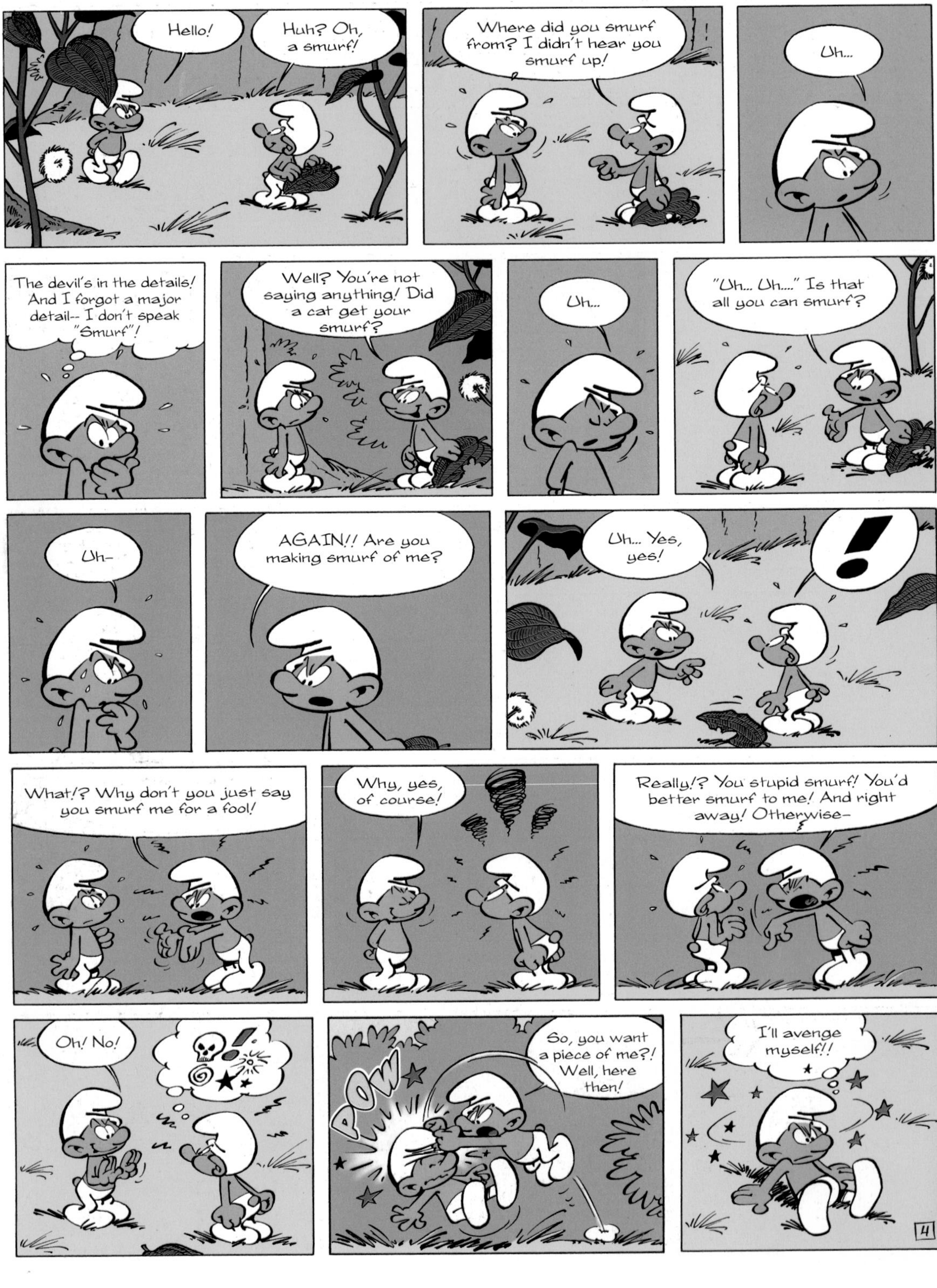

Hello!
Huh? Oh, a smurf!
Where did you smurf from? I didn't hear you smurf up!
Uh...
The devil's in the details! And I forgot a major detail-- I don't speak "Smurf"!
Well? You're not saying anything! Did a cat get your smurf?
Uh...
"Uh... Uh...." Is that all you can smurf?
Uh-
AGAIN!! Are you making smurf of me?
Uh... Yes, yes!
!
What!? Why don't you just say you smurf me for a fool!
Why, yes, of course!
Really!? You stupid smurf! You'd better smurf to me! And right away! Otherwise-
Oh! No!
!
So, you want a piece of me?! Well, here then!
POW
I'll avenge myself!!
4

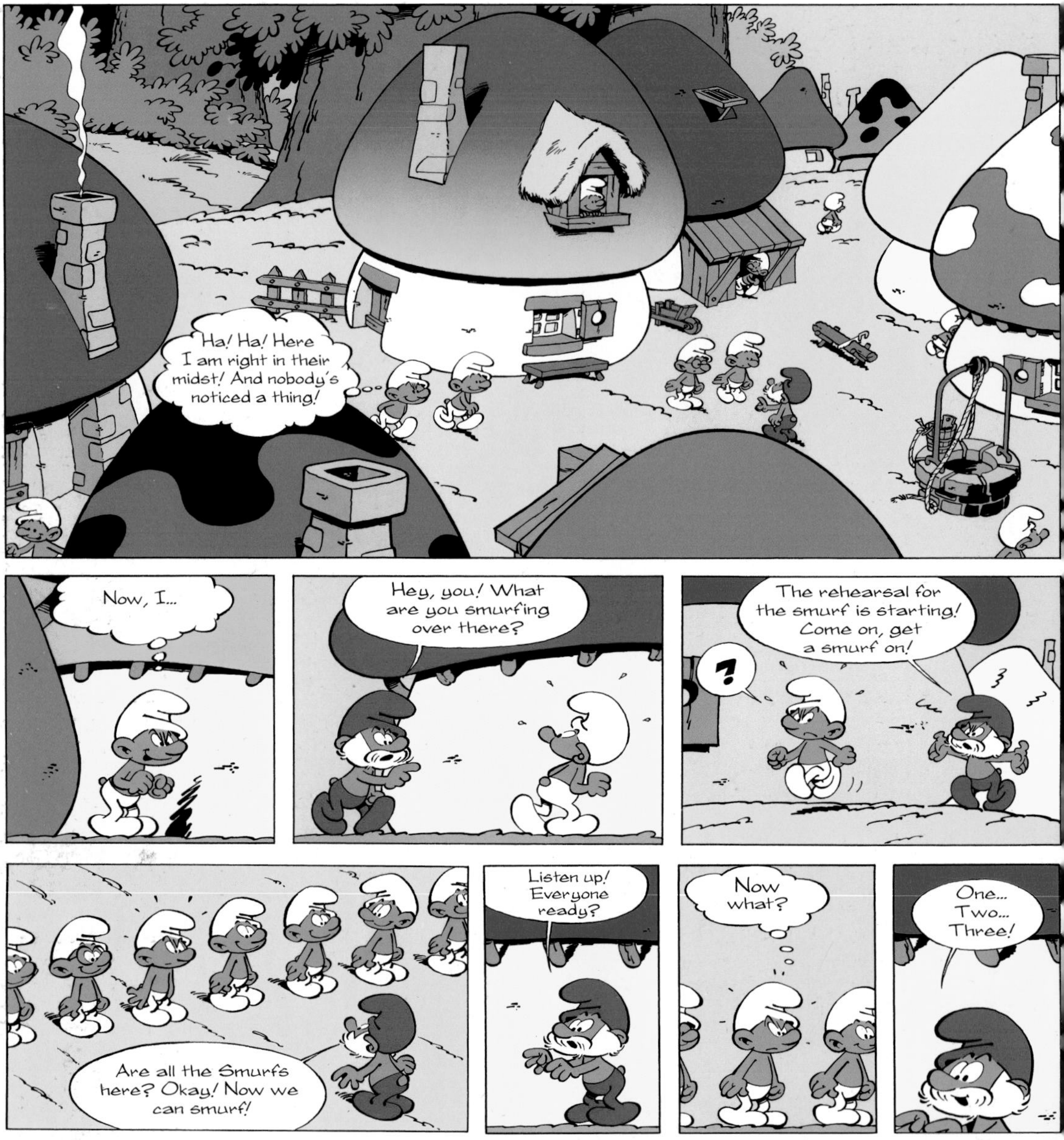

Ha! Ha! Here I am right in their midst! And nobody's noticed a thing!
Now, I...
Hey, you! What are you smurfing over there?
?
The rehearsal for the smurf is starting! Come on, get a smurf on!
Are all the Smurfs here? Okay! Now we can smurf!
Listen up! Everyone ready?
Now what?
One... Two... Three!
IT'S THE SMURF SMURF SMURF
!?
6

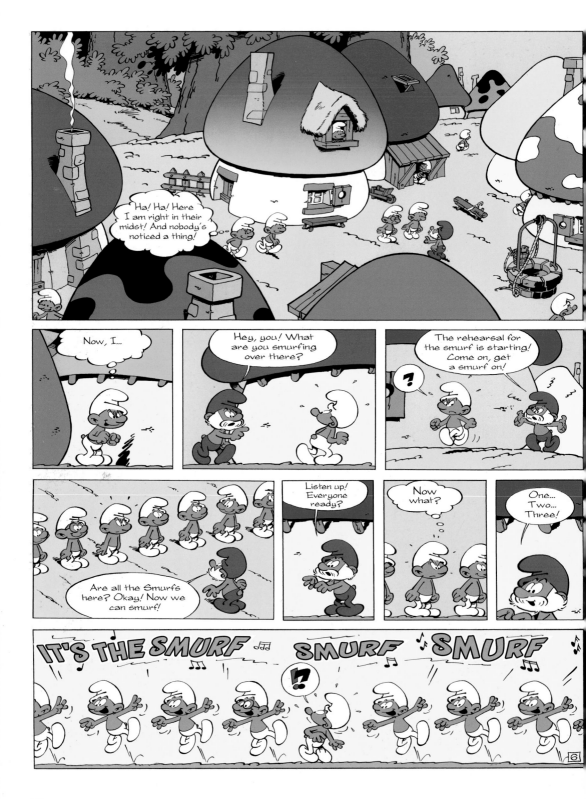

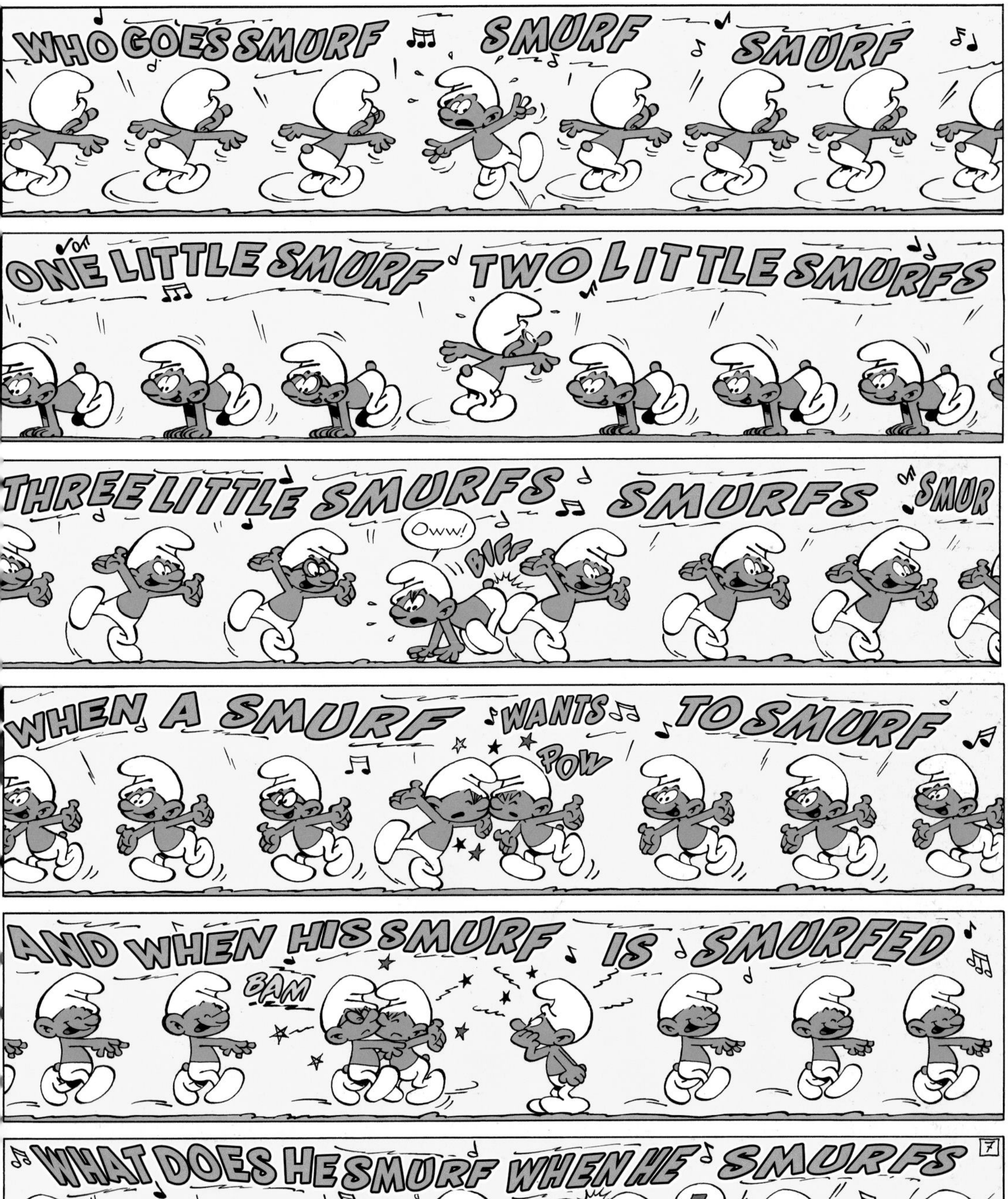
WHO GOES SMURF
SMURF
SMURF
ONE LITTLE SMURF
TWO LITTLE SMURFS
THREE LITTLE SMURFS
SMURFS
SMUR
OWW!
BIFF
WHEN A SMURF
WANTS
TO SMURF
POW
AND WHEN HIS SMURF
IS
SMURFED
BAM
7
WHAT DOES HE SMURF WHEN HE SMURFS
?

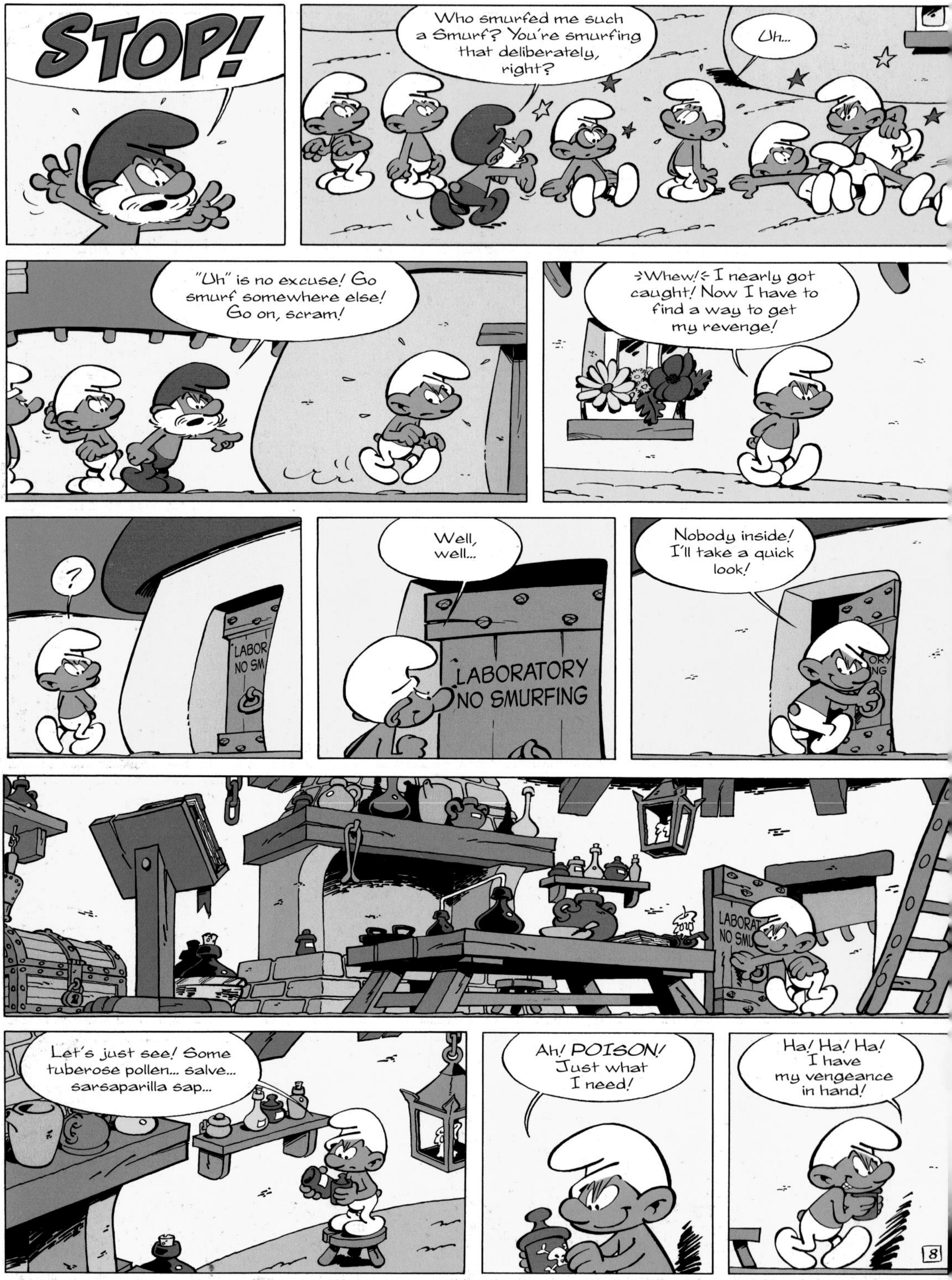
STOP!
Who smurfed me such a Smurf? You're smurfing that deliberately, right?
Uh...
"Uh" is no excuse! Go smurf somewhere else! Go on, scram!
Whew! I nearly got caught! Now I have to find a way to get my revenge!
?
Well, well...
LABORATORY NO SMURFING
Nobody inside! I'll take a quick look!
Let's just see! Some tuberose pollen... salve... sarsaparilla sap...
Ah! POISON! Just what I need!
Ha! Ha! Ha! I have my vengeance in hand!
8

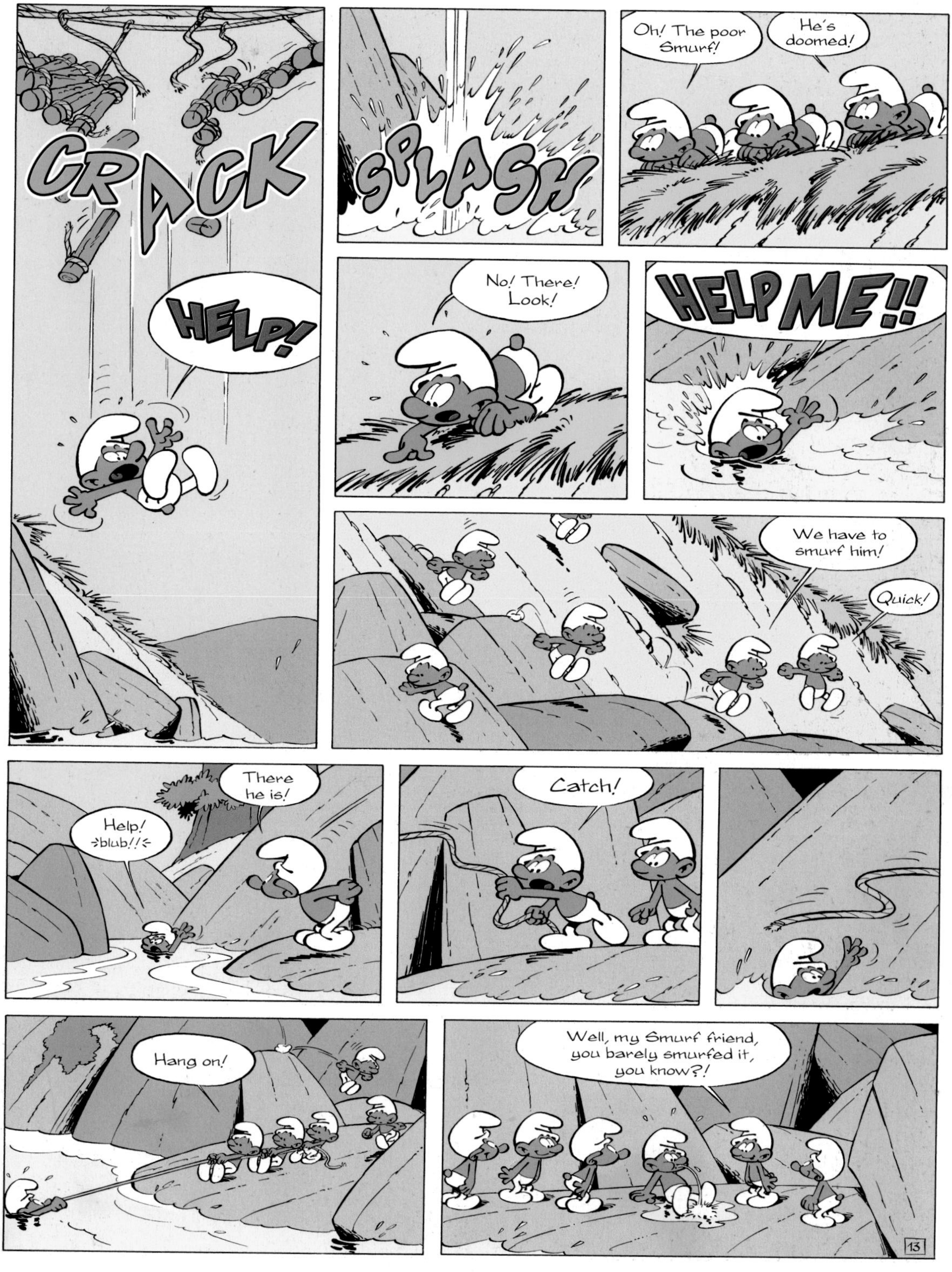
CRACK
HELP!
SPLASH
Oh! The poor Smurf!
He's doomed!
No! There! Look!
HELP ME!!
We have to smurf him!
Quick!
Help! »blub!!«
There he is!
Catch!
Hang on!
Well, my Smurf friend, you barely smurfed it, you know?!
13

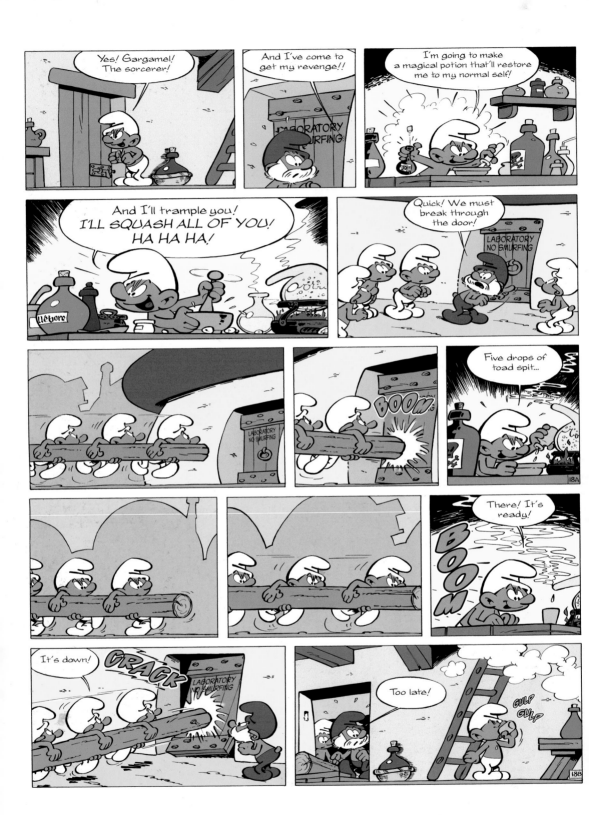

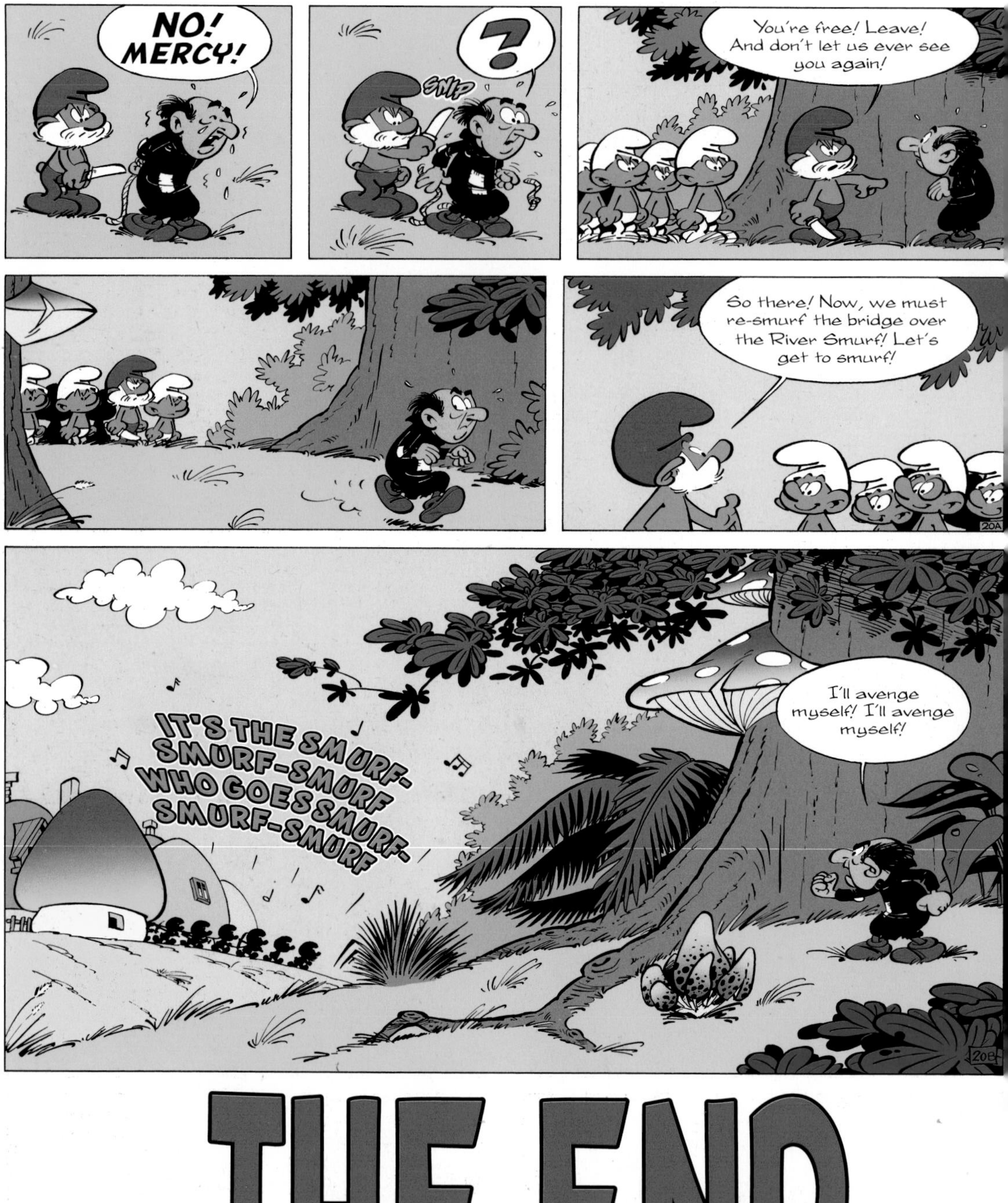
NO! MERCY!
SNIP
?
You're free! Leave! And don't let us ever see you again!
So there! Now, we must re-smurf the bridge over the River Smurf! Let's get to smurf!
20A
IT'S THE SMURF-SMURF-SMURF WHO GOES SMURF-SMURF-SMURF
I'll avenge myself! I'll avenge myself!
20B

THE END

THE HUNDREDTH SMURF

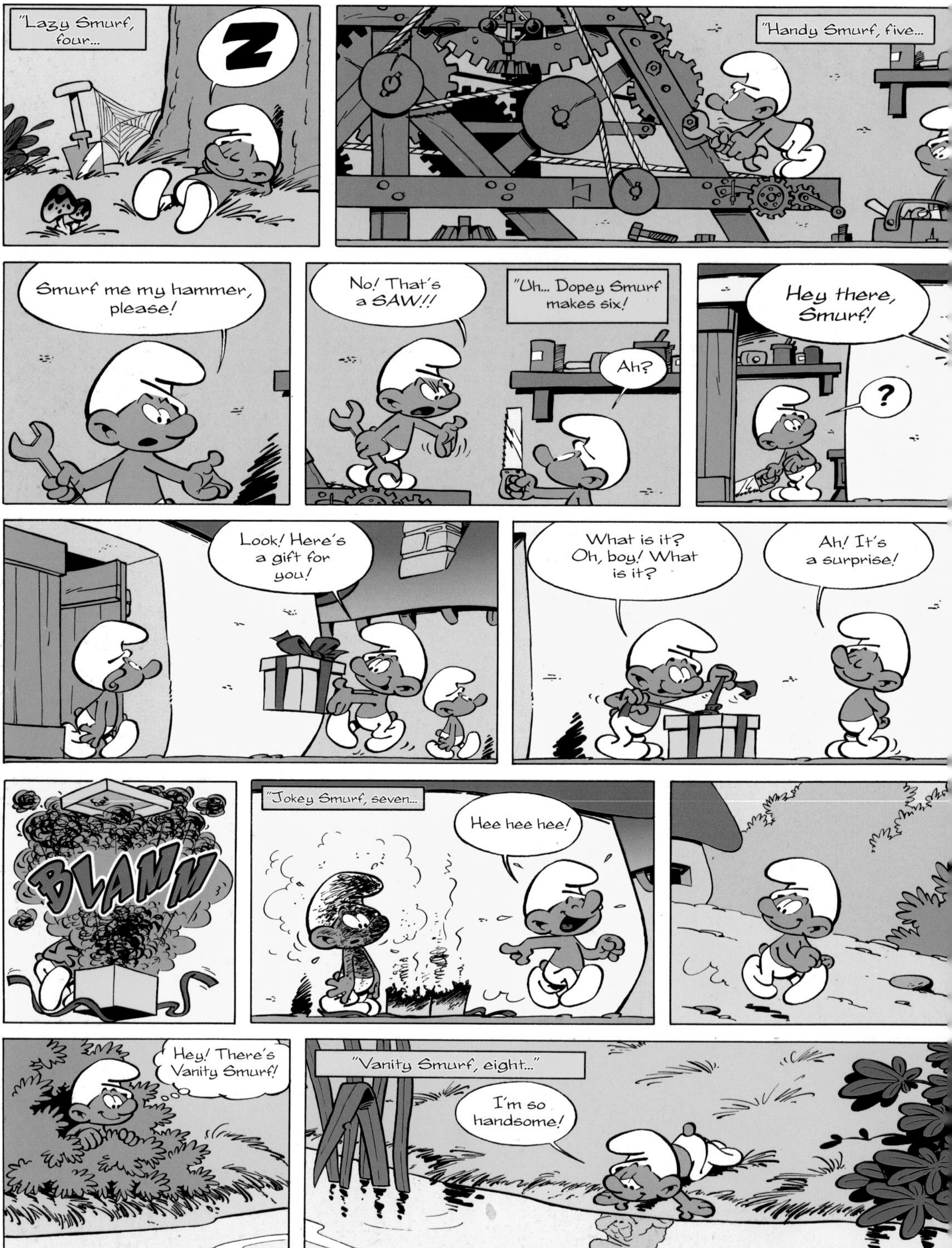
"Lazy Smurf, four...
Z
"Handy Smurf, five...
Smurf me my hammer, please!
No! That's a SAW!!
"Uh... Dopey Smurf makes six!
Ah?
Hey there, Smurf!
?
Look! Here's a gift for you!
What is it? Oh, boy! What is it?
Ah! It's a surprise!
BLAMM
"Jokey Smurf, seven...
Hee hee hee!
Hey! There's Vanity Smurf!
"Vanity Smurf, eight..."
I'm so handsome!
2

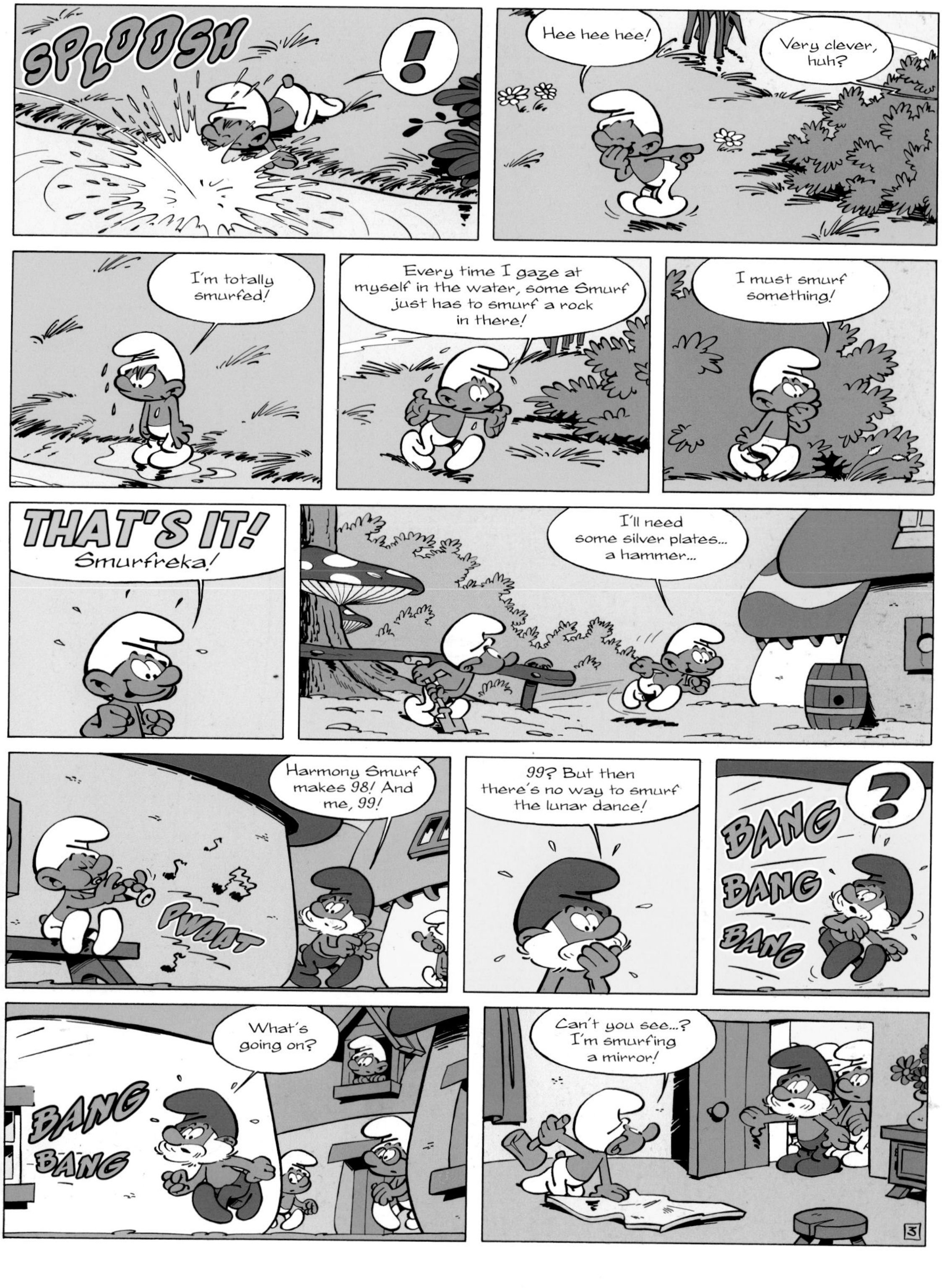
SPLOOSH
!
Hee hee hee!
Very clever, huh?
I'm totally smurfed!
Every time I gaze at myself in the water, some Smurf just has to smurf a rock in there!
I must smurf something!
THAT'S IT! Smurfreka!
I'll need some silver plates... a hammer...
Harmony Smurf makes 98! And me, 99!
PWAAT
99? But then there's no way to smurf the lunar dance!
BANG BANG BANG
?
What's going on?
BANG BANG
Can't you see...? I'm smurfing a mirror!
3

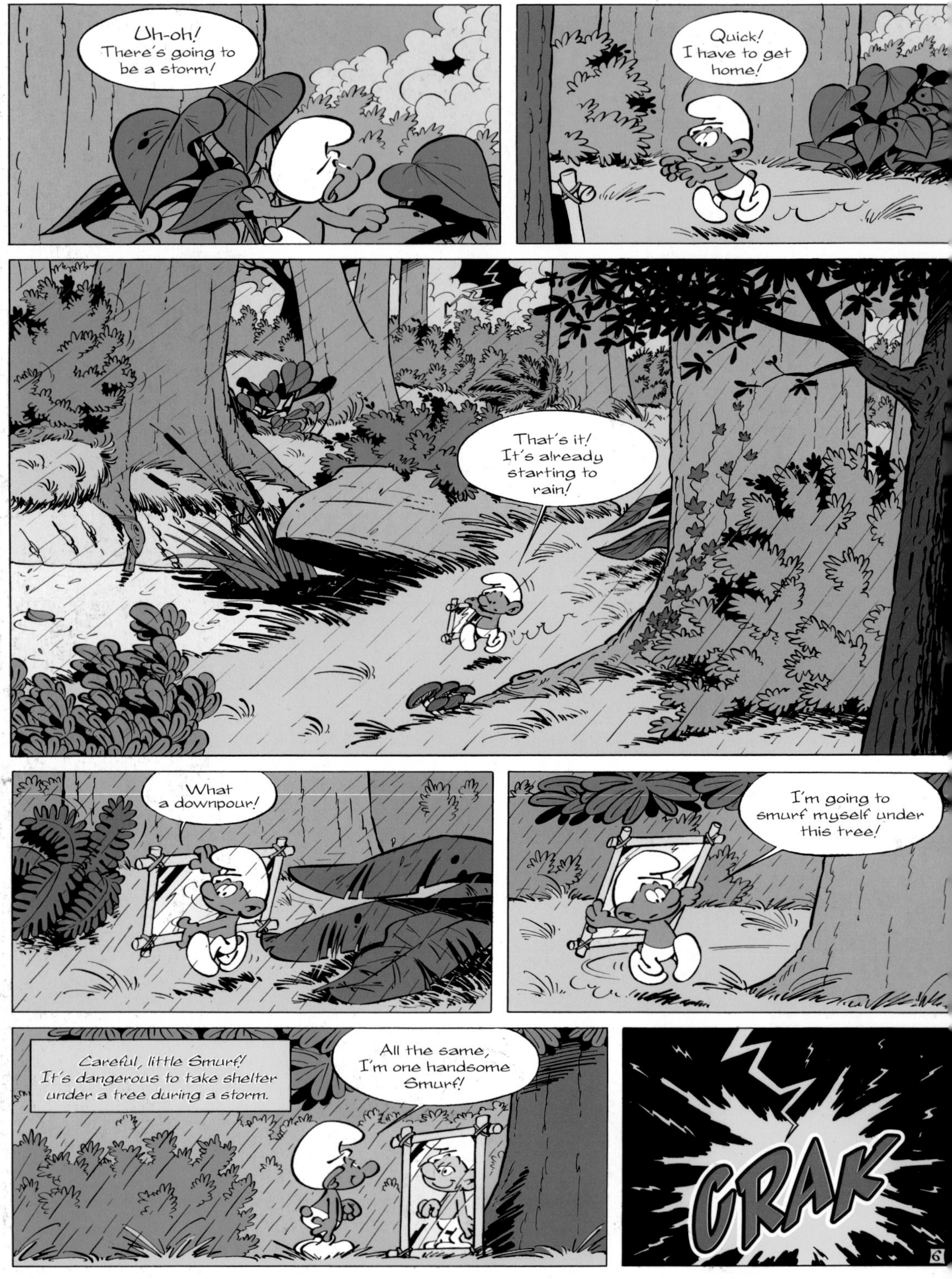
Uh-oh! There's going to be a storm!
Quick! I have to get home!
That's it! It's already starting to rain!
What a downpour!
I'm going to smurf myself under this tree!
Careful, little Smurf! It's dangerous to take shelter under a tree during a storm.
All the same, I'm one handsome Smurf!
CRAK
6

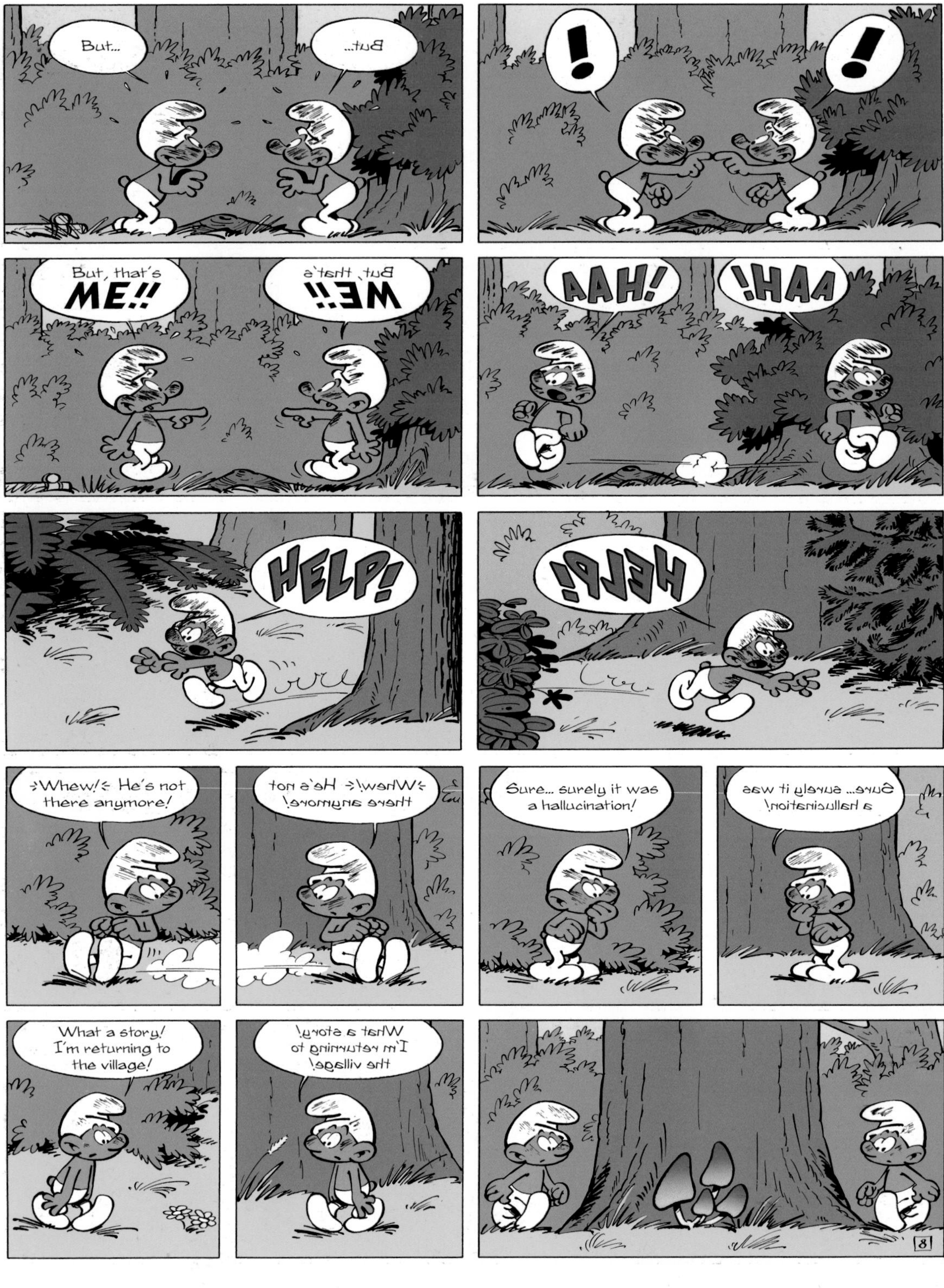
But...
But...
!
!
But, that's ME!!
But, that's ME!!
AAH!
AAH!
HELP!
HELP!
Whew! He's not there anymore!
Whew! He's not there anymore!
Sure... surely it was a hallucination!
Sure... surely it was a hallucination!
What a story! I'm returning to the village!
What a story! I'm returning to the village!
8

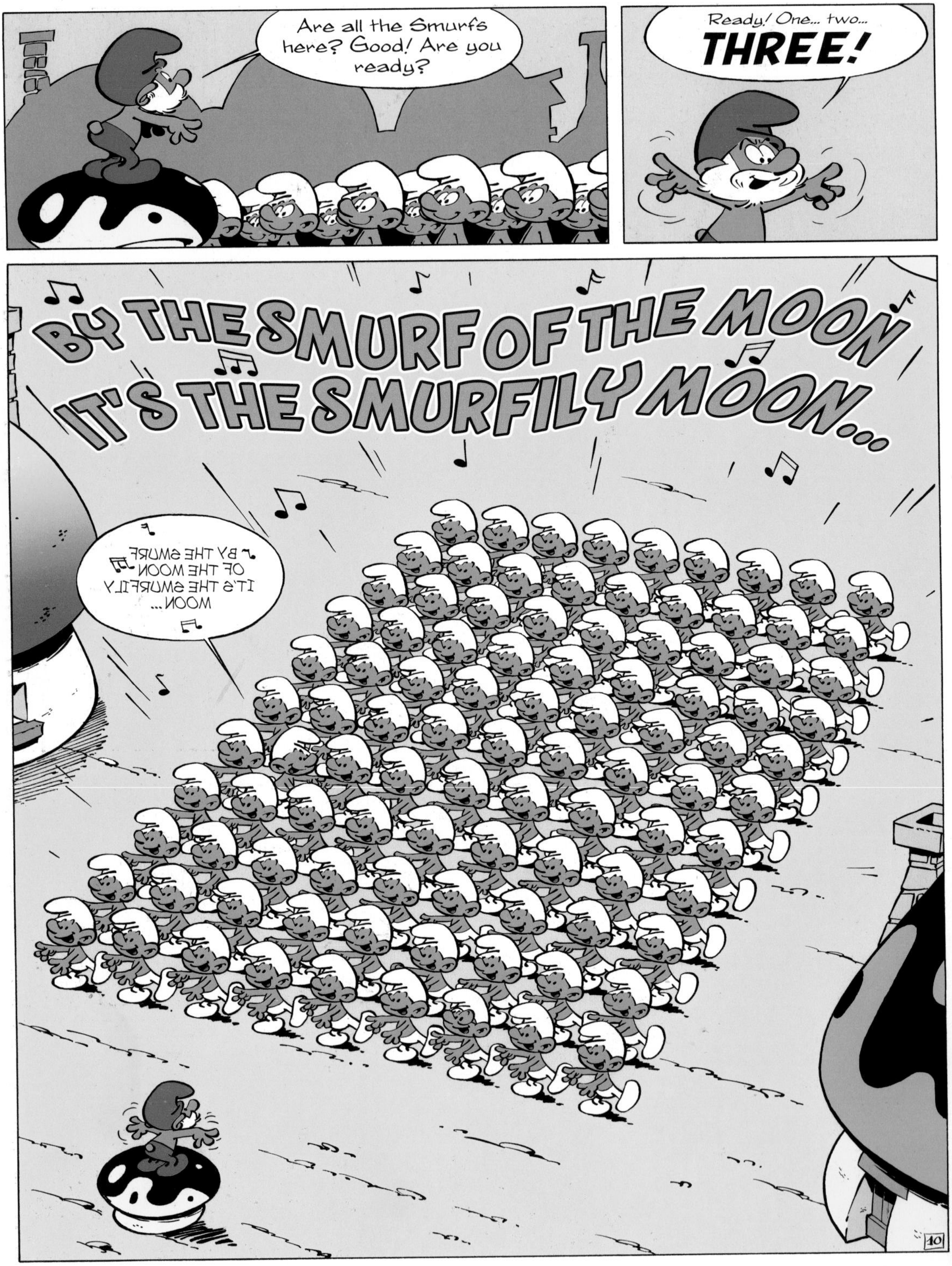

Are all the Smurfs here? Good! Are you ready?
Ready! One... two... THREE!
BY THE SMURF OF THE MOON IT'S THE SMURFILY MOON...
BY THE SMURF OF THE MOON IT'S THE SMURFILY MOON...
10

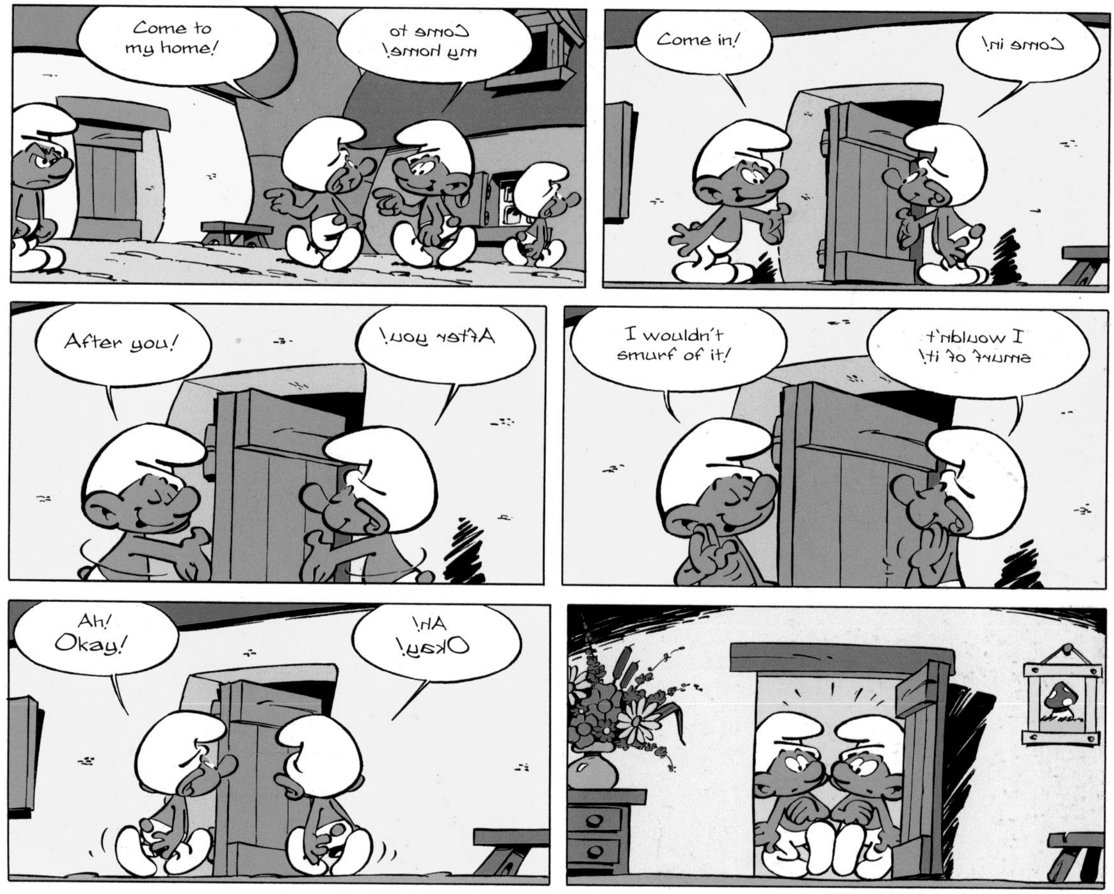
Come to my home!
Come to my home!
Come in!
Come in!
After you!
After you!
I wouldn't smurf of it!
I wouldn't smurf of it!
Ah! Okay!
Ah! Okay!
Are you hungry? I have some sarsaparilla!
Are you hungry? I have some sarsaparilla!
Let's eat!
Let's eat!
It's good, eh?
It's good, eh?

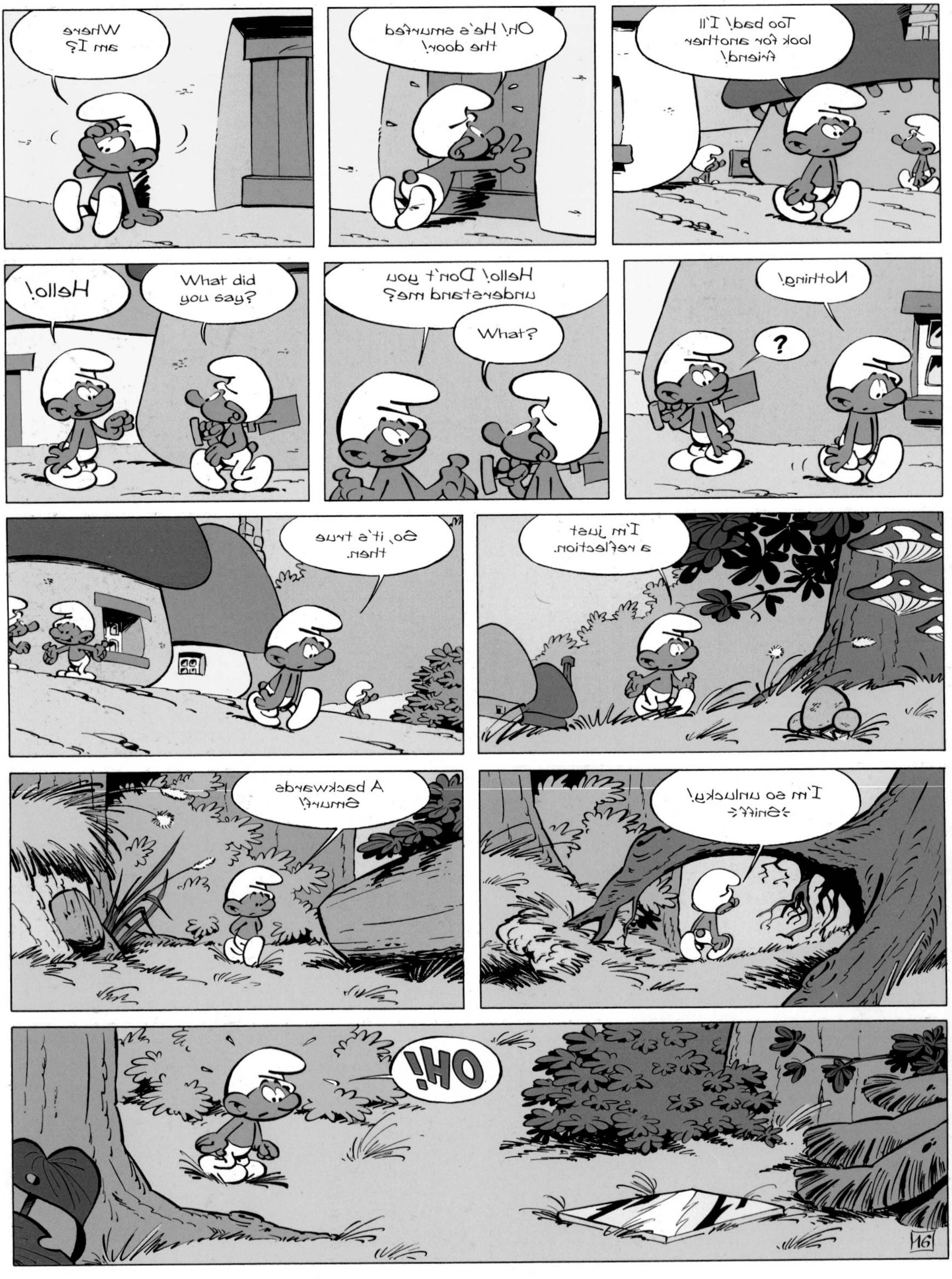

Where am I?
Oh! He's smurfed the door!
Too bad! I'll look for another friend!
Hello!
What did you say?
Hello! Don't you understand me?
What?
?
Nothing!
So, it's true then.
I'm just a reflection.
A backwards Smurf!
I'm so unlucky! ~Sniff~
OH!
16

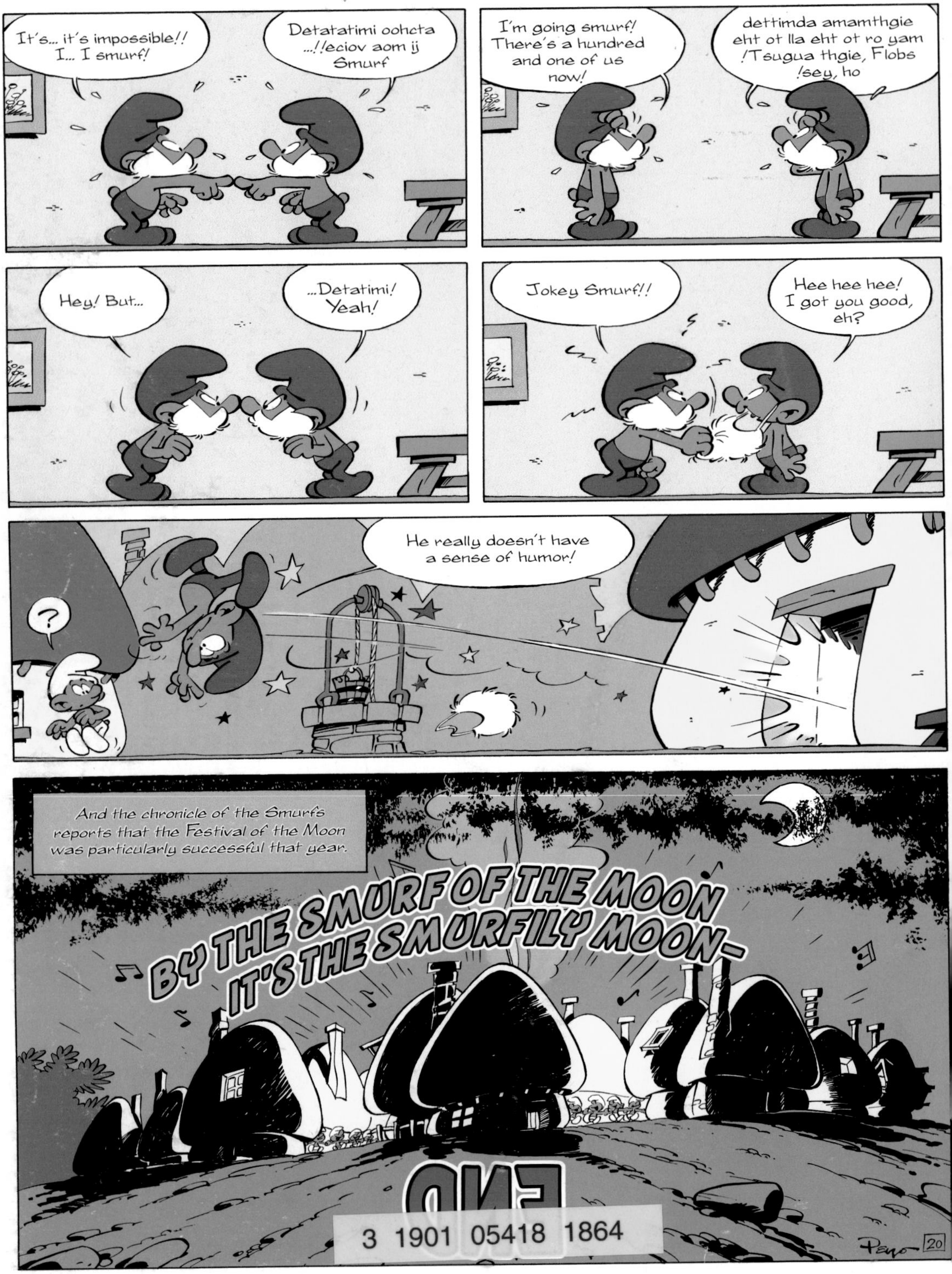
It's... it's impossible!! I... I smurf!
Detatatimi oohcta ...!!eciov aom ij Smurf
I'm going smurf! There's a hundred and one of us now!
dettimda amamthgie eht ot lla eht ot ro yam !Tsugua thgie, Flobs !sey, ho
Hey! But...
...Detatimi! Yeah!
Jokey Smurf!!
Hee hee hee! I got you good, eh?
He really doesn't have a sense of humor!
?
And the chronicle of the Smurfs reports that the Festival of the Moon was particularly successful that year.
BY THE SMURF OF THE MOON
IT'S THE SMURFILY MOON–
20